STOLEN MAGIC

SHADOW COVEN
BOOK TWO

I0773293

Stolen Magic
The Shadow Coven Book 2
Heather Young-Nichols

heatheryoungnichols.com

ALSO BY HEATHER YOUNG-NICHOLS

Shadow Coven

Haunted Magic

Cursed Magic

Stolen Magic

Fated Magic

Forever 18

Forever Grayson

Forever London

Forever Lennox

Heavy Hitter

Pushing Daisies

Daisy

Van

Bonham

Daltrey

Mack

Courting Chaos

Cross

Ransom

Booker

Dixon

Finding Love

Making Her Mine

Making Him Hers

Harbor Point

Love by the Slice

Love by the Mile

Love by the Rules

Gambling on Love

Highest Bidder

Highest Stakes

Highest Reward

Holiday Bites

All I Want

All of Me

The Fallout Series

Last Good Thing

Last First Kiss

Last Chance Love

With J.A. Hardt

Bound by Magic

With Amelia J. Matthews

Dirt on the Diamond

After Office Hours: Seducing the Professor

1

MILLER

"WHERE THE FUCK IS SHE?" I demanded as my feet hit the floor heavily.

I was pacing my parents' house with my best friends Luken McCormack and Oliver Campbell hunched over a map of the town trying to scry for my girlfriend who had disappeared.

Hazel was supposed to be at my apartment. She was supposed to be safe. I'd given her an amulet for that very thing. To keep her safe.

Yet she's gone.

"I don't know, man." Oliver shook his head in confusion. "I can't find her anywhere. So, Unless she's off this map..."

None of us wanted to say it.

There were only two reasons that a witch who

knew what he was doing wouldn't be able to locate someone by scrying and both of them burned my stomach.

Either Hazel Riley was further away than we could reach.

Or she was dead.

She better have been further away from the fucking map because the second one wasn't something that I'd live with.

"Get a bigger fucking map," I snapped.

"Woah." My dad came through the door in a rush. "That's not going to help anyone."

My jaw clench as I began pacing again, trying to contain the energy boiling inside me threatening to blow up the damn house. "Maybe not," I told him. "But what the fuck else am I supposed to do."

"How long has it been since you charge the amulet?" Dad asked as Mom joined us. The more of us the better but at the same time, I had a gut feeling that told me not to trust the council which meant I didn't want to bring them in on this.

I sighed and ran my hand roughly through my hair. "Not since Oliver, Luken, and I first did it."

Dad's jaw tensed not unlike mine had a moment ago. He and I might not have looked at all alike but our mannerisms weren't that different. Oliver and

Luken resembled Dad more than I did with their dark hair and dark eyes. We were all close to the same height but I had more of a medium blond hair and these genetic anomaly icy blue eyes. I'd seen others with them but not in my family.

"I know!" I took a deep breath trying to push down all of the feelings about to boil over. My problem wasn't with the people trying to help me. "I was going to do it last night."

"Why didn't you?" Luken asked because any tiny detail might be a clue as to where my girlfriend was.

"We were... busy." The guys all gave me a short nod because they all knew what that meant. I'd been fucking Hazel last night, thinking with my dick instead of my head. Charging that fucking amulet should've been my first priority.

Fuck.

"Shouldn't it still hold some power?" That was directed at my mom and no, I didn't give two shits that they both new about my sex life. One, they wouldn't care, and two, Hazel was more important.

"It should," Mom told us all. "But it wouldn't necessarily be enough to keep someone from getting it off her."

"What?"

"If she's wearing it, then she has a little protection. But if someone removed it…" None of us wanted to think about what that meant.

Especially since the thing hadn't been at full protective power to begin with. I hadn't known this but the night Oliver, Luken, and I made it, Oliver changed his contribution to one that meant I'd feel it if she was in danger.

I'd felt it all right but the problem was, I didn't feel anything at all now.

"There has to be something we can do." My foot hit the floor with even more force than I'd intended. "I can't fucking sit here."

"I'll go talk to Danna." Luken was already heading to the door.

"I don't want the council involved."

He turned to me. "I'll talk to her privately. You know we can trust her." Then he left.

His motorcycle roared to life then sped away from the house.

"Why not the council?" Mom asked.

I shook my head. "I don't know. It's a gut feeling." And they'd always taught me to go with my gut.

"Look." Dad brought me to a stop with his hands on my shoulders. "I know something of what you're going through right now?"

"How? How could you know?" All of my muscles

were tight all I really wanted to do was punch something. Or someone. Not him. Not any of these people in this room with me but Hazel's parents sounded like a good place to start.

Dad glanced back at Mom. "I just do. Trust me."

I was about to argue but Mom came closer. "Cooper." She laid a hand on Dad's arm which caused him to take his hands from my shoulder. "It's time."

"Later."

I had no idea what they were talking about and honestly didn't care. If it didn't have to do with Hazel that it didn't matter.

"I'm going to her house." I stomped my way to the door but Oliver slid in front of me and grabbed the handle.

"Why don't you let me do that?"

"What?'

My friend glanced at my dad then back at me. "I'll be a lot less bull in a China shop than you will be right now. I can check things out. I'll be able to get inside and check her room for anything."

"I don't want you in her room." As if that mattered.

"Miller," he said calmly moving toward me so I'd have no choice but to step back. "I can be sneaky. You're going to go in there like a fucking tornado and that's not going to get you anywhere. They hate you. They don't know me. It'll be fine. I'll call you."

Then he was out the door.

When I turned back, Mom had taken over scrying. She dangled the crystal over the map. When it started to move, a glimmer of hope sparked inside me. One that could've been dangerous given the possible outcomes.

"Let your friends help," Dad told me quietly.

Then the crystal dropped with a thud against the table and my heart fucking stopped. "Where is it?" I hurried over beside her to see the map.

"Old Midland Road?" I whispered more to myself. There wasn't fuck all out that road. No houses on that stretch that I could remember. Nowhere anyone could hide a person. At least not that I remembered. "How can she be out there?"

"She's not." Mom looked up at me with wide hazel eyes. "I changed the spell. I wasn't scrying for Hazel."

"Then what were you looking for?"

"The amulet."

My jaw tensed. We couldn't find Hazel anywhere but we'd found the amulet.

Again. There were only two possibilities as to why.

Someone removed the amulet which cut me off from her completely or the amulet wasn't on a body that was alive.

I shook my head then ran out the door.

My car engine fired with as much rage as I felt running through my veins. My tires squealed as I slammed my foot on the gas pedal.

Hazel wasn't my wife but she was everything to me anyway. For a moment I wondered what Dad meant by him knowing what I was going through but pushed that thought out of my had.

It didn't matter.

All that mattered was finding the woman that I loved.

I slammed on my breaks as soon as I got to the part of Old Midland Road where the crystal had fallen. I was out of the car almost before I got the thing in park.

As I remembered, the entire area was just fields. Now, due to the nature of scrying and the map we had, the pinpoint where the crystal had fallen wasn't exactly an X that marked the spot but more of the area.

I had to look around.

"Hazel!" I called again and again but got no answer.

As I moved carefully around the field, more cars pulled up. My dad hopped out of his truck—no Mom with him, Oliver's car stopped with Lukens bike right behind him.

The four of us spread out and slowly searched. No idea how Luken and Oliver knew what we were doing but they were looking. I moved some tall grass out of the way and my heart fucking stopped.

The amulet laid there, all alone. No Hazel. No sign of how it got there.

I didn't remember making a noise but I must've because the other three were suddenly all around me.

"Fuck," Luken muttered.

"The amulet?" Dad asked because he'd never seen it.

"Yeah." Oliver answered him because I couldn't form words.

It was laying there, the beautiful amethyst crescent moon with the tree of life wrapped around it, in the dirt. Tossed aside as if it meant nothing. Nobody made a move to pick it up. I wanted to but couldn't get my body to cooperate. My heart thudded against my chest and in my ears.

Whatever protection this thing still had, none of it would benefit Hazel. She never would've taken this off on her own.

Which meant... someone had her. Someone that could work around the amulet to get it off her.

I hope it burned the fuck out of the fucker's hand.

"Hazel's parents weren't home," Oliver told me quietly, snapping me back to what was really important.

"I'm not surprised," Dad told them. "From everything I've been told, they have to be behind this."

I leaned over and snatched the amulet from the ground. "Why the fuck has the council allowed the shadow coven to run uncheck for this long?"

"They haven't," Dad told me. "It's been a decades long game of whack-a-mole. They pop up. We beat them back. Not without casualties on our end."

"Casualties?" Luken asked.

Dad swallowed hard. "You've heard about the girls that went missing years ago. We know that was them. My sister was one of them."

"What?" My eyes snapped to his. "I thought you said she left town."

He shrugged. "She did. But it was agreed that we should keep it all quiet. She wasn't the only one."

His eyes went cold. "Your mother was almost one of them."

Acid burned my throat and my stomach churned in a way that I thought I might throw up. But there was only so much I could take right now.

"Shit," Luken said under her breath.

"Serena Good's daughter and son-in-law were killed and while we haven't been able to prove it, it was during an appearance of the shadow coven."

"That why she left?" Oliver asked. "I thought they died in a car accident."

Dad nodded. "Just another story. The more out coven members feat the shadow coven, the more mistakes will be made. They're small but strong. That's why we train you all the way we do. So you'll be ready for anything because those fuckers do sneak attacks."

"I don't give a shit about any of that," I told him. "I only care about getting Hazel back. How the fuck do we do that if we can't track her? If she doesn't' have the amulet, she's in danger."

"Let's get that back to your mom." He pointed at the necklace in my hand. "She's good with psychometry. She should be able to see what happened."

The four of us ran back to our cars and peeled out to get back to my house.

Not every witch could do psychometry but Mom could. She'd learned to control it years ago so it wasn't like every time she touched something, she saw everything. That would've driven her insane, she'd said.

But right now, it was exactly what we needed.

I didn't bother pulling into the driveway at home because based on what my mother said, I was just going to leave again. Before we could explain what we needed, Luken spoke.

"Danna didn't have much," he said. "But she did recently overhear a conversation about a deal with a dark Fae."

"Seriously?" I asked.

Oliver scratched the back of his head. "Those fuckers haven't been around here since the Fae wars. We kicked their asses and part of the truce was for them to stay away."

"We." Dad snorted but I couldn't find humor in anything. "You weren't even born yet."

"I know," he told him. "I've always wanted to meet a Fae. Light or dark I don't care."

"There's something wrong with you." Luken nudged him.

"I know but I've heard dark Fae have black hair,

pale skin, and gray eyes. Also translucent wings. Who wouldn't want to see that?"

"Me right about now," I told him because I wanted to stay focused. "What'd she hear?"

"Just that. Someone made a deal with a dark Fae because Honus was talking about it to someone, she didn't know who, and they've picked up traces of Fae in Serenity."

"Fucking humans," I muttered because they had to be the only people stupid enough to make a deal with a dark Fae. That shit never worked out.

"Yeah," Luken agreed. "She didn't have many details but telling us this shit could get her in a lot of trouble."

Honus was one of the council members. He wasn't that old, maybe my parent's age, and he was one of the better ones. He, along with Danna, seemed determined to bring the council into the new century given how old fashioned some of them were. Michael specifically.

"We won't do anything to out her," I promised. "Is she going to dig for information on Hazel?"

He nodded. At least we had someone on the inside.

"Now, Mom?" I asked.

Mom nodded then took the amulet from me. She

held it in one hand then covered it with the other. Her eyes fluttered close and watching her see whatever she was seeing was fucking torture. Dad had concern all over his face which made me wonder if he could read her in a way I couldn't. I mean, of course he could but what did it all mean.

Long moments passed before Mom opened her eyes again. When they settled on me, there were so many things behind them. The worst being pity.

I didn't want her pity. I wanted answers.

"A man tore if off her neck," she said quietly. "I didn't recognize any of them."

"Any of them?" I raged.

She quickly wet her lips. "I saw three. The two that grabbed her and the driver."

My heart was about to beat out of my chest and the rage had nowhere to go. "Grabbed her? From where?'

"Here," she said right away. "I saw her..." She glanced at Dad then back to me. "They grabbed her and put a hood over her head. They bound her hands so she couldn't do any spells."

Because Hazel was so new, she couldn't do spells like we could without her hands. That took training. Training I hadn't given her because I'd been too concerned with being inside her.

I'd failed her.

She'd been so sure that her parents weren't going to hurt her that it somehow had helped me drop my guard for a split second.

A split fucking second was all it took.

Now, she was gone and I had no way of finding her.

2

HAZEL

WHEN SOMEONE BILLED this place as like a summer camp and you knew it was going to be more like the summer camp in the Friday the 13th movies, you had to pretend to go with it.

I was being led away from the office then thrust out into the sunlight once again. I lifted a hand to shield my eyes. If there was one thing that I learned in that office it was that no one here was going to hurt me.

Scratch that. I learned that my parents were desperate to have me as part of the Shadow Coven, as Miller said, and that they probably weren't going to kill me.

But there was a lot of pain that could happen

before it leading to death and the thought caused a shiver to skitter up my spine.

As these two big goons led me through the camp, the first thing I wondered was just how big this massive wall was. I wouldn't be able to climb over it. No way. But was there another weakness?

"Don't even think about it," Goon one told me as if he could read my thoughts.

Shit. Miller had told me that there were witches who could do that and suddenly I cursed myself for not keeping a better hold on my thoughts. I'd have to be better with that. Secondly... Miller. There was zero chance he wasn't going to be blaming himself for me being taken. None.

Even though it was neither of our faults. I blamed the two people who'd created me. And why did they? Was this the whole reason? To get me here to this point?

"And don't bother hoping your boyfriend's going to rescue you," Goon two said, again as if he could read my thoughts. "Nobody's coming for you."

Goon one snorted. "I'd like to see him try. I haven't had a good fight with a light witch in a while."

"He'd demolish you," I muttered half wishing to

yell it in their faces and half knowing that it would've been asking for trouble.

"No way some lame-ass light witch could do shit."

I bit my lips together to keep from antagonizing him any further.

Right now, I needed to figure out how this worked and try to come up with a plan on how to get out of here. If only I would've taken training more seriously. Or rather, if Miller and I had trained more instead of constantly falling in bed—no. I wouldn't regret that. I didn't know what was going to happen here and my time with him might've ended up being the only good thing to happen in my life.

Because I'd said what I needed to in the office to keep anyone from doing anything rash but I'd been lying. I wasn't going to cooperate. I was going to pretend to cooperate until I could figure things out. Even being so far out of my element, there were things I could do. Or try to do.

"This is yours." Goon one pushed me roughly toward a small cabin just outside of the center of the camp. I'd guess this was where the witches were sent here to what? Train? Anyway, this area looked like it was where we'd be sleeping.

There were rows of small cabins that looked

smaller than my bedroom at home. The outside was wood but didn't look like logs and there was a small roof over the area that I'd call a porch. It wasn't really. Just a spot where you stepped before entering.

"Go in there and get settled." Goon two gave me another nudge.

"Settled? I don't have anything. Your assholes grabbed me without letting me pack a suitcase."

"Your parents brought you some things," he snapped trying hard to sound intimidating.

The two of them took a step back and I thought they were going to leave but instead, Goon one said, "Don't bother trying your magic. There are so many wards here, it'll never work."

Yeah, yeah. I'd still try it once they were gone.

They didn't leave. Instead, they kept staring at me like they were staying until I went inside. So I did.

Fuck those guys.

Three sets of eyes looked at me with curiosity. I stared back. What was the protocol here? Introduce myself? They couldn't be trusted, obviously, given that they were here. They'd be stupid to trust me. Not because I'd actually divulge their secrets to those in power but I could. And that should've been scary enough.

"I'm Nellie," the tall blonde standing next to one set of bunk beds told me. "You can have the top bunk here."

I nodded. "I'm Hazel." I didn't give her my last name because it didn't go unnoticed that she hadn't either.

She pointed to the bunk bed across the room. "They are Gia and Juniper." The young woman with the dark hair and eyes gave me a small wave but the other one didn't do much but stare.

I wasn't sure which was which but the one who hadn't waved had brown hair that was styled in a pixie cut and some of the most startling blue eyes that I'd ever seen.

Well, almost.

They reminded me of Miller's eyes. The moment I thought of him, my stomach tightened.

He must've been so worried. If he even knew I'd been taken yet.

Shit. What if he didn't know? He could've thought I just left.

So many intrusive thoughts swirled in my brain and it took a lot of effort for me to push them back.

Miller would know something's wrong. I had to trust that. Sure, I could've left but unless the assholes did something with my car, it'd still be at his house.

"Your things are here." Nellie pointed to the suitcases next to the bunk beds that I was now going to share with her. "And the bathroom is that door." Which was the only other door in the place. "Other than that, we have to go out there for anything we need."

"Out there?"

"Into the camp," pixie cut told me. "I'm Gia," she said to clarify.

"Listen." Nellie stepped closer. "None of us are here because we want to be. Looks like we already have something in common. Shitty parents."

I let out a rough breath. I'd been worried that this place was going to be filled with believers or whatever they'd be called but it looked like there might be people here that I could talk to.

"That's good to hear," I told her then realized how my words sounded. "I didn't mean—"

"I know," she said quickly. "You meant it's good that you're not stuck in this cabin with a bunch of people who drank the Kool-Aid. I get it. I worried too."

I moved over to my suitcase and eyed one of the closets. My parents had packed one small back and I was sure that when I opened it I'd find absolutely nothing I would've packed for myself.

"You can use this closet." She tapped her fingertips against the wooden wardrobe on the left side of the beds. "I have my stuff in the other one."

"Thanks," I told her.

The four of us grew quiet so to have something to do, I leaned the suitcase over and unzipped it. Surprisingly there weren't dresses and skirts inside but jeans and shorts. Maybe this one time my parents had gotten it right.

Slowly, I began to move the clothes to the wardrobe. I figured that I was going to be here for however long and I'd need to change. If I found a way to escape, I'd leave it all behind. I didn't care.

"How long have you all been here?" I asked as I carefully hung up a shirt. This job should take as long as humanly possible because once I was done, all I could do was stare in silence.

"Two days," Nellie answered first.

"Juniper and I came in together a week ago," Gia told me as she swung her legs over the side of her bed. "We were friends before this. Our parents were friends."

Nellie flopped onto her stomach on her bed.

"How long have your parents been trying to get you into the Shadow Coven?"

I shrugged. "My whole life, I suppose. I only found out that I was a witch recently."

"They bound your powers?" Juniper asked with surprise.

"Yeah. They weren't the ones to tell me. If they had it their way, I probably still wouldn't know."

"Who told you?" Nellie asked.

All of these questions so far were rather benign. Normal getting to know you shit if you could call witches and a shadow coven normal. And kidnapping. That was what they did.

"My boyfriend Miller." There was no reason not to tell her. Even the assholes who'd taken me already knew that. I hadn't said anything my parents or anyone else didn't know.

"How'd he know?"

I turned to face her. "He's a witch. He wanted to train me so that this—"I flapped my hands to indicate everything—"Wouldn't happen. Guess it didn't work."

"Aww... " Juniper's voice was soft like she found it dreamy. "Do you think he'll come rescue you?"

"Like a knight is shining armor?" Gia added.

I snorted. "Knowing Miller, it'd be more like

Godzilla with a hand grenade but yeah. I'm sure he's trying to figure out where I am."

"The three of us have known we were witches our entire lives," Nellie explained. "We didn't know we were being raised in this though and when it came time to commit, we wouldn't."

"What do you mean?" I sat on the one chair in the room which happened to be in the middle of the beds so we could all see each other. Juniper hopped down from her bunk and sat beside Gia.

"You have to commit yourself to the Shadow Coven. Express fealty or what the fuck ever. But... I didn't want to. I've grown up seeing what these people do, or some of it anyway and I want no part. That earned me my spot here."

"What is here?" I asked because I still didn't have a clear picture of what I was doing here other than it having to do with my parent's coven.

"I call it the brainwashing camp," Gia offered."

"Excuse me?"

"Yeah," Juniper agreed. "Parents send us here so that the Shadow Coven can convince us to choose the dark." She shivered. "Not all of their methods are pleasant."

I raised my eyebrows. It was about what I'd figured but hearing it was insane.

"How old are all of you?"

"Eighteen," Juniper and Gia answered at the same time then chuckled.

"Nineteen," Nellie answered.

"I'm nineteen, too." It was nice to have these girls in my cabin and that it seemed like we'd be fast friends. "So is everyone here so they can convince us to join them?"

"Pretty much," Gia told me. "There are some our age here that have already chosen the Shadow Coven but now work as a fucked up mentor to us all. To show us how great it is."

"But it's not," Juniper told me.

"I didn't think so."

Nellie sighed. "The dark magic does a number on you. Use it long enough and it messes with your brain. Turns you dark and these people... they kill, they steal, they destroy anything in their paths and right now, we're in their paths. We're not with them so we're against them and I think that even if we never agree to be on their side, they'll keep us here if for no other reason than to ensure we won't join a light coven. I'd had the fucking chance and I hesitated. That's how I got here."

I would've joined Miller's coven in a heartbeat but I wasn't ready. I didn't know the craft well enough to make that decision. Now I wish I would've anyway.

"What was your mortal sin?" Gia asked. I furrowed my brows in confusion since I didn't know what she was talking about. "The thing that made your parents act. The thing that made them bring you here."

"Oh." I tucked a piece of red hair behind my ear. I must've looked like an idiot or at least someone who didn't brush their hair regularly given what I'd just been through. "Fell in love with the boy who hated me in high school."

Nellie smiled. "I feel like that's something I want to hear about."

I snorted. "Miller told me I'm a witch. Then he showed me I'm a witch. He and his friends were training me to use my magic." I glanced around. "I don't suppose it'll work here, will it?"

Nellie was already shaking her head. "They've got it warded to the fucking hills. The three of us have been testing areas to see if there's a weakness but so far, we haven't found one. But they also don't give us much time to do that."

After thinking about that for a bit, I wet my lips quickly. "Well, now you have someone else to help you look."

Nellie gave me a grateful smile. "Do you shower in the morning or at night?"

I furrowed my brows. "I'll shower any time but I prefer to shower at night. Wash the day off me why?"

"Gia and I are morning shower people. Juniper prefers night. This just makes it balanced."

And I guess that in a situation like this, balance was probably the best I could hope for.

"You know," Gia broke the silence that had formed between us. "If we could find a weakness in their wards, you might be able to connect with your guy mentally. Send a telepathic message."

"What?" That wasn't something I'd ever been able to do or ever told anyone could do other than those that could apparently read our minds. "You can do that?"

Juniper glanced at Nellie then back to me. "I did it once when I was visiting family in Mexico. I wanted Gia to know how unhappy I was. It worked but I didn't try it again because not long after we ended up here."

"But you could teach me how?"

She nodded. "Probably. If you can really ground yourself. But we have to find a weakness first."

"I'm in," I said quickly. "Whatever we have to do.

If I could let Miller know where…" my voice trailed off. "I don't actually know where we are."

"Doesn't matter." Nellie pushed to her feet before making her way over to me. "That just means we have more than one thing to do. Figure out exactly where we are and find a weakness. There has to be one. But I have to ask one thing before we put our necks on the line."

I waited, my heart pounding against my chest in anticipation of what she was going to say as well as with hope that maybe all is not lost.

"If they come for you, you have to take us with you. You can't leave us behind."

"I won't." That was an easy deal to make.

I'd just met these three young women but there was no way I was going to run without them.

Together we could be strong. Together we could fight.

Together, we just might not end up in the dark coven at all.

3

MILLER

WHEN I'D FELT Hazel's fear, it came with a heaviness in my chest that felt like someone had parked a Buick on it.

Right now, I'd give anything to have that feeling back.

At least then I'd know she was alive.

Rage causing me to come out of my skin had replaced the heaviness but this wasn't good enough. Not until I got my hands on either her or the person I needed to kill to get to her.

Make no mistake.

I was utterly homicidal at a level that I'd never thought I could reach. That was naive to think and it'd only been because I'd never loved someone like I did Hazel.

"You look about to come out of your skin," Oliver said as I paced my parent's house again.

Mom hadn't gotten anything else from the amulet so right now she was in my apartment probably touching everything she could get her hands on to see if she could get a reading. Then they'd try Hazel's car.

"That's because I'm about to come out of my fucking skin." Everyone could see it. I could feel it. There was no reason to try to deny it.

"I wonder if your mom sees... *everything*." That was Oliver's way of trying to lighten the mood but the joke was on him. I didn't want it lightened.

"Fuck off," I snapped at the same time Luken told him, "Not the time."

The back door opened and shut with a thud meaning that my parents were coming in. My mother had to have found something. Anything. I didn't care how small it was. I was desperate.

"Well?" I pounced as soon as they came through the door.

"I'm sorry, Miller." Mom's chin dipped to her chest for a moment. "I didn't find anything useful."

"Useful? Did you see anything?"

She shifted uncomfortably. "I did see some

things, of course, but nothing that could help us here."

"Fuck!" I raged. Not at her but this entire situation. I was a caged animal about to strike out at the people trying to help me and I couldn't do that. We were all in danger from the Shadow Coven and everyone was doing the best they could.

"What'd you see then?" Oliver asked and everyone could hear the humor in his voice.

I swore then and there that I was going to murder him.

Mom shook her head. "Nothing I'd like to share."

The fact that my mother might've touched my best and seen me fucking Hazel didn't even matter to me. I wished that I could touch it and see the same thing. Anything that could remind me of her.

"We've got to go to the council," Luken said before I could lash out at the people who loved me the most. "Danna said they're calling a meeting. We should all get official alerts in a second."

As if on cue, all of our phones dinged with a message that I didn't bother looking at. We already knew what it said so fuck it. I turned for the door.

Each of us took our own cars, or in Luken's case motorcycle. I couldn't be cooped up in a small place with anyone else right now. I needed the space to stew in my absolute rage at the situation I currently found myself in and I needed time to convince myself not to let my thoughts go dark. They already had but I guess they could've gone darker.

Those people could've been doing anything to Hazel. Anything. They'd raped members of our coven once. They took some of the young women.

Fuck.

Oliver had told us once that he'd heard about young women in our coven who'd been impregnated and taken. Dad didn't confirm the impregnated part but he had the taken part. But if that was what the shadow coven was up to with Hazel, I was going to kill every single one of them.

Danna was out front, ushering everyone inside. Our coven wasn't the largest but it was the oldest and the strongest. Or it used to be. Seems like before I was born, when Serena Good was in charge, we'd been stronger.

"What's with the meeting?" I asked Danna in no mood to sit in a fucking room with these people right now.

"Michael wants to calm the fears of the coven." Danna Payne had her usually long dark hair pulled up into a bun and looked like she'd either been sleeping or the day had exhausted her.

"Calm the fears?" I snapped.

"Yeah. He says there are rumors circulating that there's been a shadow coven attack but all of our intel doesn't back that up."

"You know that's bullshit."

"I do." She glanced at Luken probably because he'd been the one to go to her after Hazel had been taken. "But listen." She wet her lips quickly. "I don't have time to go over it right now. Let's get this over with then meet at my place. Something isn't right here."

Yeah. No shit.

Mom and Dad joined us right then. Oliver's mother was already inside but he didn't go sit with her. Luken didn't have anyone else so he stayed with us as we took our seats.

Michael's presence brought a hush over the group.

"I've heard the ramblings," he started while looking across the room directly at me. My jaw tightened. "The council has checked all of our defenses and every single ward is unmarked." Because if one of the wards the council placed to protect the town had been breached, there would be a dark mark on it.

If Michael was so fucking powerful, like Serena had been, why the fuck were we still dealing with these bastards in the first place.

Yes, shit had happened under Serena's watch, but most of that had been in places that weren't protected or with magic that the wards didn't cover.

It was almost impossible to plan for everything.

"We are all still safe. I'm not sure what caused the rumors to swirl—"

"Hazel Riley," I called out.

"What?"

After pushing to my feet, I folded my arms over my chest. "Hazel Riley is why the rumors began."

"Hazel and her parents aren't part of the coven so I'm not sure—"

"Her parents are Shadow Coven."

Michaels's jaw tensed as a murmur went over the crowd. My guess was that he didn't like to be interrupted but I couldn't give a fuck. He had to be lying.

"Miller Campbell, that's an accusation that no one will take lightly." He spoke to me but Danna's leg began to bounce. There was something more happening here and if I got into too big of a pissing match with Michael, I'm liable to be here all night.

"Hazel's gone," I told him because I couldn't help

myself. There was a stabbing pain in my heart when I mentioned her name. "Taken."

Michael shook his head. "Again, Campbell, you have no proof the shadow coven is involved. To accuse in such a manner will just cause panic."

Danna caught my eye and shook her head so slightly that most probably wouldn't have noticed it. She wanted me to shut up and sit down.

There was definitely something else going on.

I didn't care about any of it unless it had to do with Hazel.

Instead of arguing with him and proving to him that the shadow coven is in play here even if he didn't want to admit it, I sat down. To the confusion of both Oliver and Luken.

My knee bounced until Michael was done speaking and the meeting ended. I hurried my ass out of there like it was on fire with my parents and the guys right behind me.

"We have to go to Danna's," I told them as soon as we were out of the council house.

Oliver shook his head and asked, "Why?"

"She said to." I looked to my parents who were standing there with us. "You two should go home. Search for something else for us to try."

"We'll check every spell book I have," Mom

assured me. She gave my arm a squeeze before the two of them walked away.

"You don't want them to go to Danna's with us?" Luken asked. "They might know more about whatever she's going to tell us."

"No." I shook my head. "Because after her house, I'm breaking into Hazel's house. They don't need to be there for that." I turned and headed to my car. It took the two of them about ten seconds to run after me.

"Break into her house?" Luken asked as if it was something we did all the time.

It wasn't like it was hard but we hadn't done that. We'd chosen the light and all the good shit that came with it which meant using our magic for good, for protection. But the way that I saw it, getting into that house was part of protecting Hazel.

"Yup. I'm going to find something. I can't sit around and wait for... whatever."

"We'll go with you," Oliver said right away and I'd known that was going to be the case.

He'd been to the house but I didn't think he'd been inside. We were going and I wasn't going to stop until we found something.

First, the three of us met at Danna's and waited outside her door for her to arrive. Her car came to an abrupt stop at the curb then she hopped out like she was being chased.

"Get inside," she called then flung her hand which caused the door to her place to spring open.

The three of us stepped inside. She followed seconds later then flung her hand again. The door slammed shut and all the locks turned on their own, securing us inside.

"Is someone chasing you?" I asked her.

"No." She was out of breath and holding something in her hand as she turned on some lights. "I just don't want anyone to see you three here."

"We're really not that embarrassing," Oliver joked.

She scowled at him. "I didn't mean that. I meant I didn't want anyone to see us meeting after just leaving the council."

"What's going on?" Luken asked stepping up to her.

She stopped, took a deep breath, then blew it out slowly.

"OK. So..." She began walking toward her kitchen causing the three of us to follow. Whatever she had to say was important enough to her that I didn't want to miss a word. "I've been noticing that something has been weird with the council recently.

Or forever." She set the folder down on the island then yanked the refrigerator open to pull out a bottle of water. "Anyone want anything?"

After a round of no's, she continued. "I can't be sure of any of this but I've suspected that someone hasn't been working as hard for us as he says. That he hasn't been casting the ward the way that he says."

"Michael," I spat through clenched teeth.

"Who else?" She shook her head. "If he finds out we're having this conversation you know he's going to want me burned at the stake."

"They don't do that anymore," Oliver countered.

"Oh my sweet summer child," she told him then patted him on the cheek. "Making accusations is basically treason and I'm not making an accusation. However, I went out to the west land marker a couple of days ago—"

"Alone?" Luken asked with a tight jaw.

I didn't think there was anything between the two of them but all of us were friends. Any one of us would've gone with her. If she'd been caught double checking Michael's work, she wasn't wrong. There would've been hell to pay.

"I was fine. Anyway, someone mentioned that something was off out there so I went to look. She pulled her phone out of her pocket. "The wards had been breached and not replaced."

"Whoever set them would've felt them breached," I told her.

"Michael set them."

"So that fucker's not even trying to protect us?"

She sighed. "He has most people convinced that he is protecting us. Anyway, it's not just the wards. He goes off on these meetings with other covens except when I speak with them, they have no memory of a meeting with him. But he's doing something."

"Why the fuck do we all trust him?" Oliver asked as he slammed his fist on the island.

"I don't," Danna and I said at the same time.

"I don't anymore," she clarified. "He took over the council in an unusual way and the more I dig, the more I discover things he's not doing according to our sect. It's like our rules don't matter to him."

"What do you mean took over the council in an unusual way?" I asked. The guy had always given me the creeps, but I couldn't put my finger on it.

She drained some of her water and took a breath. "Twenty-one years ago, Michael just showed up. Out of nowhere. Somehow, that earned him an immediate spot on the council. All I could get from some of the older members was that he'd saved some witches lives. It wasn't until I reached out to Serena Good that I found any real answers."

"Fuck," Luken muttered. "She's still alive?'

Danna snorted. "Yeah. She is. She's raising her granddaughter. Anyway, she didn't want to talk to me because she's left the life behind her but I begged. I told her the things that I've found. So she explained."

Danna took another breath while the other three of us waited. A dark pit formed in my stomach at the idea of what I was about to hear. Somehow, I knew it was going to involve me, or what's going on with Hazel.

"Michael showed up twenty-one years ago," she said quietly as if she was afraid someone might over-hear us. "Out of nowhere. But he protected a couple of our witches who'd just had a baby. I mean had the baby that day. The shadow coven wanted that baby, apparently, and even she wouldn't give me all of the details on that. Said I'd have to ask those witches." Danna quickly wet her lips. "But he came back with them and immediately wanted on the council. Soon after, Serena's daughter and son-in-law were killed in what they say was a car accident."

"Wasn't it?" I asked.

She shrugged. "Serena wouldn't answer that question. Anyway, it was clear she had to leave to take care of her granddaughter."

"Which left her spot on the council open," Luken filled in the blanks. "And because she was the head of the council..."

"Michael slipped right in."

"Are you saying," I began. "That the shadow coven killed her daughter so that Michael could take over?"

Danna swallowed hard and shook her head. "I'm not saying that. Yet. I'm doing more digging."

Luken shifted. "You're putting yourself in danger."

She nodded. "I don't care. There's so much more I haven't found. I know it. I'm not stopping."

"Wait." Oliver tapped his knuckles on the counter. "Why don't we ask the witches he saved? They'd know where he came from and why the fuck he needed to save them, right?"

"They would," she agreed. "But..."

"But what?" I asked.

"It's your parents, Miller. It was the day you were born."

I stumbled back a step like she'd reached out and punched me in the gut.

Fuck me.

"I guess I need to talk to my parents."

4

HAZEL

THE FOUR OF us had fallen into an easy chat and if I was better at convincing myself of things then I'd think I was at a normal camp. Though I'm way too old for that. I was about to ask how the whole thing worked outside of this cabin, as in, where did we eat? What did the shadow coven do to try to convince us to become one of them when Nellie sat up straight with wide eyes.

"There's one thing that's most important," she told me as she grabbed my hand. "You're a virgin."

I snorted. "What?"

"Yeah, at some point, they're going to make you pledge that you're a virgin and it doesn't matter if you are or not, you need to say you are. It's this whole purity thing and I don't know why it's important."

"That's true," Juniper added. "When I was processed, there was another girl who said she wasn't a virgin." Her dark eyes met mine. "We've never seen her again."

Well that was... confusing and the height of patriarchy. "What about the boys?"

Gio shook her head. "No. They don't need to be virgins."

I snorted. "Figures. But wouldn't telling them you're not a virgin be a ticket out of here?"

"No." Juniper wet her lips. "I don't know what happened to that girl but I feel certain she wasn't just released to go home. They were pissed."

"I think," Nellie butt in. "That the virginity thing is just for here. Like I've seen other's pledge to the shadow coven and the use of dark magic and I know for a fact they weren't virgins."

"Ok." Though it didn't totally make sense to me. "I'm a virgin no matter what."

Before any of them could speak again, there was a knock at our door. Nellie took a deep breath and stood. "What happens in here, stays in here. It's the only way to keep the four of us safe."

"Absolutely," I whispered back as the other two nodded.

Nellie went to the door and when she opened it, a tall man with russet hair, who didn't look much older than me, stood in the doorway.

"Caleb," Nellie greeted as she stepped aside.

He didn't enter the cabin but she waved her had so that the three of us hurried over there.

"I'm here for you, Hazel Riley," he said causing my heart to race.

"Me? Why?"

"You're assigned to me and I need to show you around."

I glanced at Nellie with the unspoken question of who this guy was and why I was supposed to go with him. She gave me a quick nod that I hoped included the promise to explain everything later. I stepped forward then Caleb motioned for me to come with him.

"I'm Caleb," he told me again.

"I heard Nellie say your name."

"Right."

We began walking to our right which I already knew would lead us back to the main area. What I had seen of the place, it was set up within the high walls that reminded me of a fortress. There was the main area that I'd only gotten a brief glimpse of before and then the cabins were further out. Maybe so we could sleep through any noise. I didn't know.

"What did you mean by me being assigned to you?" I asked. Caleb walked with some distance between us but was absolutely close enough to reach out and grab me if I made a run for it.

Where would I go anyway?

"You were assigned to me. I'm one of the assistants here."

"Like a camp counselor?"

I would've sworn that a smile played at his lips but he never let it loose. "If you want to call it that. I'm in charge of you and your cabin mates. My job is to usher you through this process as easily as possible. Make sure you follow the rules and stay out of trouble." He stopped and turned to me. "Which reminds me." He scratched at the back of his neck. "It's also my job to get you to declare your purity. Your parents have assured...people that you're a virgin."

My skin burned, but I hoped he wouldn't see it. "Yup. Big old virgin here."

His eyes narrowed but then he nodded. "Good."

When he turned to keep walking, I had to jog to

catch up to him. "Is there going to be a test or something?"

"No." He snorted. "First, there's no physical test that can tell if a person is a virgin or not and the spells we've tried have been... imprecise."

Good. Not even their witchcraft can out me. I'm safe then though I hated having to lie about Miller in any way.

Miller. I'd done a decent job of keeping my mind off him for at least a little while because when he did creep in, all I could think about was the hell he was probably going through. He wouldn't know where I was or if I was all right.

"So." He came to a stop in an open area. "This is the main area. This is where you'll train and where you'll eat. You shower in your cabin but pretty much everything else will be here."

"Train?" I asked because I'd already been training with Miller.

"Yes. Your parents bound your powers. They're still bound actually until they decide to remove it which I'm assured will be before you commit to the shadow coven." I swallowed hard. "The downside of being bound is that you can't come into your full powers until the unbinding but you can still learn. You can still use the craft. Now, I know this might be scary since you didn't even know you were a witch until recently and the thought of doing a spell is daunting. It's my job to make sure it's not."

Wait. That means the shadow coven doesn't know that I was training with Miller. They don't know that I've already learned some things.

And if I have my way, they never will.

As I thought it over while Caleb showed me around, it made sense. There was no reason for the shadow coven who practices dark magic to know anything going on in the light coven.

At least for now, my secrets are safe.

"Any questions?" he asked.

I glanced around and realized that he'd taken me back to my cabin and I'd missed everything he'd said or shown me due to being lost in my own thoughts.

"I think I'm good. If I missed anything the girls can fill me in." I went to go inside but Caleb's hand shot out and wrapped around my wrist.

"Remember, anything you do to break any rules or step out of line from this point forward will result in your whole cabin being punished." He stepped in so close that I could feel his breath on my face. "I really don't want to have to punish any of you, ok?"

Something inside me, something Miller probably would've called my witchy sixth sense, told me that Caleb was being sincere. He didn't want to have to come down hard on us so we all needed to make sure we didn't give him a reason.

"Got it."

He released my arm and I went inside the cabin, falling back against the door after it shut.

"That was quick." Juniper was on her stomach on her bed swinging her legs back and forth.

For some reason, those three didn't seem nearly as concerned as I was. After all, Juniper and Gia had been there one week longer than I had which feasibly meant that they'd be forced to declare themselves earlier than I had been.

"I remember almost none of it but he did tell me that the four of us are basically a unit. If one of us gets into trouble then all of us do."

"Yeah." Nellie came out of the bathroom and flopped into the chair. "They told me that shit too. I think they think we'll all behave so that the others don't get into trouble."

I took a breath and wet my lips. That's what I was afraid of. I needed to work on getting the hell out of here and in doing so was well aware that I'd be breaking rules and probably getting into trouble. However, I didn't care. The risk was worth it to get back to Miller. I'd pretend to be on board, to want to become one of the pod people, until I escaped. However, there wasn't a doubt in my mind that when the time came, if it was the only way to keep Miller and his family safe, I'd pledge to the shadow coven and the use of dark magic.

"It does present a problem," I told them as I climbed up to my bunk and dangled my legs over the side. It was high enough that I could've reached out and put my hands flat on the ceiling.

"Why?" Gia asked. "Planning to escape."

I raised my hands to show that was exactly what I was planning to do.

"There's no way to escape," Nellie told the three of us. "I haven't tried everything, of course, but..." She glanced at the three of us as if she was deciding how much to tell us. We may have only known each other a day but we were in this together now. "I overheard some things when I was coming in. This place is locked up tight but I assume there has to be a weakness."

"There usually is." Gia swung herself around so that she was sitting on the very corner of her bunk. "There's one thing we all need to agree to. If any of us are doing this, we're all doing it because we're tied together. Maybe between the four of us we could figure something out."

After wetting my suddenly dry lips, I decided to tell them about Miller and what I hoped he was doing. "I have a boyfriend," I said bringing all of their attention to me.

"Yeah. Me too." Nellie snorted. "I don't know how that will help."

"Is your boyfriend a powerful member of a light coven?"

Her eyes widened. "He is not. My boyfriend is an adorably clueless human who probably thinks I've ghosted him by now."

"Wait." Juniper dropped off her top bunk. "Your boyfriend is a witch? But you didn't know you're a witch?"

I furrowed my brows. "Why do you think I didn't know I was a witch?"

"I heard them say you're bound. You don't have powers."

I blew out a quick breath. "Yeah. I didn't. Until Miller showed up at the bookstore one day and told me I'm a witch." That was the pared down version of what happened but still. "Then he trained me. Or started to train me."

Juniper took three more steps toward me and hung onto the metal edge of the bed. "You're telling me you've had training? But you're still bound?"

"I guess."

"Calm down, Juniper." Nellie shooed her back a little. "Even with bound powers, we can still learn spells and shit. We still have the craft." Her brown eyes with specks of gold turned directly onto me. "It just means that she has another power, one passed down from ancestors that her parents didn't want her to have full access to."

"I don't think that's it."

"It has to be," she insisted. "You don't have your full powers but I'd bet whatever they're trying to hide is still leaking out."

My top lip curled over my teeth. "Leaking? That doesn't sound appealing."

She giggled then hopped up next to me. "It's the best way I can describe it. I grew up knowing I was a witch. I knew that my parents were dark magic and when I was old enough, I refused to pledge my fealty to the shadow coven. I wanted to be normal. That pissed the parental units off and here I am. So I've learned things. I can help."

Juniper suddenly looked nervous. "Are you saying that there's a chance we might get out of this? Out of here?"

"I don't know," Nellie told her. "But I'm willing to try if you three are."

After a murmur of agreement, I was now in an escape pact with three girls I'd met hours ago. Whatever it took to get out of here.

"First order of business…" Nellie hopped off the top bunk and landed on her feet like a cat. "We're not prisoners in our cabin. We can go out. I say we wander around to a far corner and see if we can get a message out."

"A message?" I furrowed my brows.

"Yeah." Her face saddened. "It's unlikely to work but we could try. You have to know how to ground yourself really well. Which, I don't know about any of you but my parents did not focus on teaching me that."

Before I could ask why, Gia leaned closer to me, "The more you can ground, the more powerful you are so dark witches tend to wait to teach that until after their kid has pledged to darkness."

Hope sprung in my chest. Hope that I hadn't felt since that asshole grabbed me at Miller's apartment.

"I know how," I told them. "I know how to ground myself. Miller taught me. He was insistent that it was the first thing I learn."

All of their eyes widened.

"I'm not sure I'm great at it but I know how to do it."

"Let's go as soon as the moon comes up."

It took hours of us anxiously waiting but as soon as we could see the sun in the sky, the three of us headed out. We walked and walked and walked looking for an open area. According to Nellie the more moonlight we had on us when we tried, the better it'd be.

The sky darkened and moon brightened as we made our way as far from our cabin and anyone else as we could.

"They don't have people out here?" I asked once we stopped.

"I think they have people who run the perimeter every so often," Gia explained.

"Run the perimeter? Are we in a movie?"

The four of us giggled quietly.

"No." Gia looked up at the moon then back to us. "But they have heavy wards out here. Why would they need security?"

"OK. Let's do this." The sooner I could possibly reach out to Miller, the better.

"OK." Nellie stepped into the circle Gia, Juniper, and I had unintentionally formed. "Make sure your face is up to the moon, ground yourself as you know how, and think about him. I assume that's who you'll try to reach out to. The rest of us don't have anyone."

I nodded and did as she said.

My face was up toward the moon and I allowed myself to relax into the ground, feel the energy. Once the energy vibrated beneath my feet, I pulled the way I'd always tried to do.

Miller. Please hear me. Please hear me, Miller.

There'd be no way for me to know if he received the message or not but I had to keep trying.

Miller. I'm with the shadow coven. Please help me.

5

MILLER

"To your parents' house?" Luken asked as we all stood there, me trying to make sense of what Danna had just told us.

The story of Michael saving witches and being brought into our coven was true. OK. That seemed fine but to find out it was my own parents and technically me since it was the day I was born. That was too much.

Not once had my parents told me about this and as far as I could tell, they weren't friends with Michael. Friendly, sure. We all were. He put in decades on our council making sure that the coven was safe. But I'd think if he literally saved our lives we'd all be... I don't know. Closer.

"No," I told them which brought curious looks. "I want to check the bookstore and Hazel's house first."

"Meet you there."

Luken and Oliver headed to their cars but I hung back. "You want to be there? When we talk to my parents?"

She wet her lips quickly. "Yes, but it could be a personal story so you can just let me know what they say about Michael. If you're comfortable."

I gave her a curt nod and stomped off to my own car.

Fuck I was antsy. Ready to crawl out of my skin because Hazel wasn't with me. I'd killed before. Enemies of the coven. The dark witches right before I was sent to Hazel were the last but over the years there were others. A shifter. A... you know what? It didn't matter.

Right now, I was ready for the blood of whoever was holding Hazel and I was going to find them.

The bookstore was closest so that was where I went first and thankfully, Oliver and Luken had made the same assumption. They were waiting for me out front. It didn't seem that any of us was worried about someone seeing us.

I didn't care. I needed to find Hazel.

After climbing out of my car, I began walking to

the door with the two of them behind me. I flicked my finger and the locks disengaged. It wasn't hard to break in somewhere at all. Not when you knew what you were doing and I knew what I was doing.

Not every witch could perform every trick and honestly, most were content to stick to nature spells, or whatever. I wasn't content with that and now it was paying off.

"I'll check the back," I told them then headed to where I knew the break room was.

"I'll check the office." That was Oliver and I trusted him to be thorough. That left Luken out in the main area.

I pulled things out of every cubby but didn't find a single thing of hers. It was like she didn't leave any shit here. But there was nothing clue wise as to where she was or who had her other than us knowing it was the shadow coven. I needed a fucking name and had hoped her phone would be here.

Nope.

"Anything?" I asked when I came back out.

Both told me no at the same time so we headed to her house. Fuck. I hoped her parents were there.

They weren't. It was better for them that way but I needed something to take this damn energy out on.

Another finger twitch and the three of us were in the house.

"Let's start upstairs," I told them.

I went straight into Hazel's room. Fuck. It smelled like her. This strawberry vanilla aroma filled the room. While I wanted to tear the place apart, these were her things so I'd take care. But I could hear Oliver and Luken not being as careful in the other rooms.

"You almost hit me with that," Luken griped.

"You ducked in plenty of time," Oliver countered.

I was glad they could take this with such ease but it wasn't the woman that they loved in danger.

It wasn't a surprise when I didn't find anything. She didn't know about this shit so there wouldn't have been anything in her room. I knew that. Deep down I thought I only wanted to check here because it'd make me feel closer to her even if only for a moment.

I did. But all it achieved was pissing me off more. She should've been with me right now. Her soft skin against mine. I never should've let her talk me into getting her shit alone.

All of this was on me.

And I'd die trying to get her back.

"Anything?" Luken asked when I gently shut Hazel's door.

I shook my head but couldn't speak right then. Being on the verge of breaking the fuck down meant that if I told him that I hadn't found anything, I'd fucking lose it.

"Let's go downstairs." Oliver led the way.

Downstairs wasn't going any better until Luken started tapping on the walls. "Does that sound right to you?"

"It doesn't." We'd all heard the hallow vibrations when he knocked. "There's got to be something back there."

"Makes sense," Oliver agreed. "If Papa Riley has anything he wanted to hide, he'd hide it. He's a witch for fuck's sake. It's got to be a cloaking spell or something."

I nodded. "Good thing I was always and expert at finding my birthday presents," I told them.

They took a big step back because they had to know that I was going big. I held up my hands, and mumbled the words I knew I'd need and the bookshelf started to shake. Nothing else was moving so that was where the entrance was.

"Fucking idiot," I said under my breath then

pulled my hands toward me which pulled up the bookcase to reveal a hidden room.

The three of us had to step over the books that were now on the floor but I didn't give a fuck if her parents discovered that we were here. Honestly, I wished they'd come home and surprise us right now.

They wouldn't leave alive unless they told me where Hazel was.

The three of us went to work pulling shit off shelves, and opening drawers. I had no idea how long we were there before I found a secret drawer.

"I'm guessing dark magic ain't shit," I told them. "Or he's just shit at it."

"Or you're really good with your magic," Luken countered.

It wasn't that. Either of them would've been able to find this shit as well.

It took strength to overpower whatever was holding that drawer shut. It wasn't magic. My guess that he thought the room was hidden so he didn't have to hide anything else.

He was wrong.

I pulled out three ledgers, handing one to each of them then taking one for myself.

"It's an account ledger. Or whatever," Oliver told me.

"Mine, too," I agreed. But that didn't even make sense. "Doesn't everyone bank online now?"

"Fuck," Luken muttered. "Not if you're trying to hide something." He flipped his ledger around so that the both of us could see it. "Those aren't numbers. Those are names." He ran his finger down the list. "Hazel's specifically."

My stomach turned. He was right. Hazel Riley jumped from the page, mocking me with the fact that I had no idea what this list was about.

"Why is there a B next to her name?" Oliver asked.

"No fucking clue. No idea what this list even is." Even after flipping back to search for a note or heading or something, we found nothing.

"The interesting thing is," Luken began while flipping the pages to the front of the book. It made me want to punch him for making it so I couldn't see her name. As if that was actually her. "There are a few things here that I think can help. A couple of addresses. One is repeated a few times."

Oliver and I went back to our ledgers to thumb through the pages quickly. That same address appeared in my books three times and his four.

"It has to be where she is. These have to be shadow coven ledgers. Otherwise why would these names be in here?"

"I agree." Luken let the ledger close.

"We have to go." I grabbed the book and stomped toward the door.

"Woah. Wait a minute." Oliver slid in before me.

It'd been almost the whole day since I'd kissed Hazel goodbye this morning. The sun was setting and I was getting anxious. I hadn't thought it a real possibility that I'd go the night without her. What if it was days?

Fuck. I felt sick. The vomit threatened to climb my throat but I wasn't going to let it.

"Get the fuck out of my way," I barked. "I'm going."

"Oliver's right." Luken was suddenly blocking my way along with our friend. "We have to plan. We should go talk to your parents about what Danna told us and about this. If you run off half-cocked, you're going to get killed."

"I don't fucking care." I pushed forward but they didn't budge.

"You'll get us killed too."

"What?"

"If you go, we're going with you. That's how this

works, man. But we need a fucking plan, Miller." Luken sighed and ran a hand over the back of his head. "I know you want her back—"

"You don't understand shit."

"In this case, you're probably right but that's why you have us here. To keep you level-headed."

"We need to talk to your parents," Oliver pushed.

They were right. I knew they were. If I was going to get Hazel, me alone fighting the entire shadow coven wouldn't go well. I'd probably get her killed so as much as it went against everything my head and my heart were screaming at me to do, I relented.

"Fine. Let's go to my parent's house."

Oliver pulled out of the driveway first then Luken waited for me. It was like they were escorting me because they didn't believe I was going to my parent's house. I was. They'd gotten through to me but I swore to myself that the moment I could, I was going to check out this damn address.

"Mom!" I yelled as soon as the three of us came in the kitchen door. Oliver went to the fridge to get himself a water then slid one in front of me. "Dad!"

Mom and Dad came into the kitchen quickly. Mom looked worn out. My guess was she'd been trying since we left to scry or use her psychometry to help me find Hazel.

"I found Hazel's phone," Mom said sliding it over the counter to me. I slammed down on it with my hand. "I couldn't get anything off it though. It's almost like something is blocking me."

"Blocking you?" I asked. "Has that ever happened before?"

"I don't think so." Mom hadn't always been able to use this particular gift. It had shown up later. After I was born, she started seeing visions when she touched things and now, she can control it so her entire life isn't taken up by other people's life. Once in a while, usually when there's a danger, the vision will breakthrough even when she didn't intend for it to.

"It's got to be the shadow coven," Luken offered. "We don't know much about them so we don't know what kind of shit they've tapped into."

6

MILLER

"Yeah." I swallowed hard and turned the phone in my hand. There wouldn't be anything on it that would give me a clue but I knew that if I turned it on and when to her photos I'd see her beautiful face smiling back up at me.

"Miller." Oliver nudged my arm.

"Right." I choked back the emotion that I didn't want to deal with right now. "We found something at the Riley's and Danna did some digging and came up with something."

"You know we'll help you any way we can." Dad sat on the stool at the island and waited.

"We found this ledger. There's an address inside that repeated in other ledgers as well as this one. We're pretty sure that her dad was doing the books for the shadow coven. Or that's what it looks like." I slid the book over to him and ignored the fact that I didn't want to say her name right now. I'd lose my shit. "We think that could be somewhere they're holding her."

Dad flipped through, nodding as he took it all in. "Why is there a black B next to Hazel's name?"

I swallowed hard. "I don't know. Her parents wanted her in the coven pretty badly. More than I'd say is normal for parents who just want their kid to follow in their footsteps."

"So you think the B represents exactly why they wanted her there?"

I shrugged my shoulders because none of us really knew anything. "It's a best guess."

"Right." He ran his finger over her name and the B. "We'll need your mom to do her thing." He glanced over at her. She held her hand out but he wouldn't give her the book.

Mom looked exhausted with dark circles under her eyes and eyes sagging. She was pale. This was the look of a woman who had overextended herself. When a witch uses a power that isn't a spell or potion it puts a drain on their system. Or it does in most cases and certainly when using something like my mother's.

She'd told me once that her visions felt like she was living what she was seeing. So she had to live her life as well as someone else's or multiple other people's. It took a toll and sometimes, she needed to recharge.

"Cooper," she nudged.

Dad glanced at me then back to her. "I think it can wait a minute."

"Cooper! Let me help my son."

Fuck. Dad almost never refused Mom anything she wanted. He was going to give in and if this went too far, Mom could be irreparable damaged and with her energy so low, it might not even work anyway.

"It can wait a bit," I told her but the words felt like acid on my tongue. I didn't want to wait a second. "We have something else to talk about."

Dad stood then moved mom over to the stool basically forcing her to sit down. Her shoulder slumped forward as he got her a drink. She'd been working hard since I'd left.

"I'm going to be straight with you," Luken began. "We don't trust Michael."

Dad furrowed his brows and folded his arms over his chest.

I needed to take this over. These were my

parents. "We found out that he hasn't been charging the wards to keep the shadow coven away."

"What?" Mom asked with confusion. "That doesn't make sense. He's always protected the coven."

I shook my head. "Not always. They're charged but not strong enough wards to actually keep people protected. I think that's how the shadow coven got Hazel so easily. We didn't even know they were there because we didn't have the wards. If they'd blackened, we would've known."

Because once a ward is crossed, which was rare but could happen with the right kind of magic, they turned black. That was how you knew someone was around that wasn't supposed to be.

Mom dropped her head into her hands. "That doesn't make sense."

"Danna has been digging. She knows that the stories we've heard were true. About the women being drugged and raped then kidnapped. We also know that Michael showed up the day I was born and saved us. What did he save us from?"

There wasn't much I knew about when I was born outside of the same things everyone knew. My parents were so happy, etc.

Dad took a step forward and placed his hands on

the counter then locked gazes with Mom. She gave him a slight nod.

"When I told you about the woman, about my sister, there was something we left out." Dad swallowed hard like this was the last thing he wanted to tell us. "My sister was one of them, that's true. But so was your mother."

I swayed on my feet like he'd physically shoved me.

"Fuck," Luken muttered but otherwise the two of them were silent.

"So not everyone got pregnant and obviously they didn't take her so..."

"I did get pregnant," Mom said quietly then looked up at me with tears in her eyes. "Your dad got me out of here before they could get to me. We spent the pregnancy in a cabin in the woods. The day you were born, the protection spell broke and we were attacked. Michael showed up, killed the dark witch, then came to Echo Valley."

There was far too much information swirling around in my head. "But that would mean..."

Dad's gaze locked with mine and his jaw tensed. "I'm your dad, Miller. That's not going to change."

Fucking hell.

Not only had the shadow coven hurt my aunt and my mother but my father wasn't even my father.

"Then who..."

Mom shook her head and swallowed back her tears. "We don't know. I don't remember anything of that night so I haven't been haunted by it. But your dad... he protected me. He was there for me. It was just him and an old witch midwife when you were born."

"So you two weren't..." Together was what I wanted to say but I couldn't get the word out.

Dad came around the island and put his hands on my shoulders so I'd have no choice but to face him. "Miller, I'd loved your mother for years before this happened but we were friends and I didn't want to fuck that up. Then everything happened and there wasn't a chance in hell I was going to let something happen to her or let her go. She was mine before this, I just hadn't said it. But this..." he squeezed a little harder. "This means nothing. Nothing changed. I'm still your dad in every way that counts."

Fuck. It was a lot to take in but it didn't change anything about how I felt about my parents. My dad was my dad. He was right.

But now the murderous rage that was already

part of me exploded. I wanted to get my hands on anyone who'd hurt my mom. Not my spells.

My fucking hands.

Dad gave me a tight hug and when he released me, I knew we needed to move. I'd bury some of what I was feeling right now because we needed to get to Hazel. She had to be the priority. Nothing could change for my mother but they could be doing the same thing to Hazel right now and I couldn't live with that.

"OK." Dad slapped his hands together. "Let's focus on Hazel right now. You can't run off to this address, Miller. We need to be smart about this."

"I know." But first, I went to my mom and gave her a big hug. Nothing they'd told me changed how I thought of her and I wanted that to be clear.

Luken and Oliver had stepped back, giving us a little privacy though they could still hear everything. Now they stepped back up.

"We need to check this out and I don't think you should be the one to do it." I opened my mouth to argue. "Miller, you're going to see something and instinct is going to take over. Normally that's a good thing but for this, we need a plan. I'll go check this out. Oliver can come with me. You and your mother should get some rest. She's not going to be able to help if she doesn't get it."

"I'll fill Danna in on what we've learned," Luken said quietly then turned to my parents. "If that's OK with you."

"Yes," Mom told him with a nod. "If this is going to help Hazel in any way, absolutely tell her. I'd rather not everyone know but a lot already do. They were there."

Luken put a hand on Mom's shoulder and squeezed reassuringly. "Danna will be discrete. I only want to fill her in because something's going on with the coven and she's helping us. Which puts her in danger too."

"I understand." Mom patted his hand before he let go.

"Fine," I bit out. "But I'm not going to be able to sleep."

"Rest," Dad said. "We'll be back as soon as we can."

Oliver patted my back as he passed me to leave the house with Dad. Luken was right behind them.

Mom remained in awkward silence for several seconds before she spoke.

"I didn't want you to ever find out," she said quietly causing my stomach to tighten. "Not because it means anything about you but because your dad is your dad. I didn't want you to question that. He loved you since before you were born. There was never a question to him that you're his."

"I know, Mom." My voice was quiet as I fought the emotion of what she'd said. "It doesn't change anything. I fucking hate that you went through it."

Mom smiled and while it was a tired one, she meant it. "At least I don't remember it. It hasn't affected my life the way it could have."

I furrowed my brows. "I'd saying having a baby so young affected your life pretty well."

She snorted. "Yeah but it was with your dad so I didn't think about it that way."

Those two shared a love that I'd never considered I'd have but I knew, right as I stood in that kitchen that if Hazel came out of this pregnant, that kid was mine. And I'd kill the motherfucker who made it happen.

"Go lay down, Mom. Dad's orders."

Mom sighed but pushed herself off the stool, kissed my cheek then headed upstairs to bed. It was likely going to be ten hours before she'd wake up. I'd never seen her so worn out in my life.

After snagging Hazel's phone off the counter, I headed into the living room and dropped down on the couch for my mandatory rest period that pissed me off. I wanted to be getting my hands dirty. Needed to be actively trying to find Hazel. Fucking something.

But I was resting.

I pressed the button to wake her phone up and stared at her lock screen. It was a picture of the two of us smiling up at the camera. I'd taken that picture and my hand tightened around the damn thing. This was going to be torture.

Since I knew her code, I opened the phone, checking emails, texts, and everything. There was nothing surprising there which was what I'd expected.

Then I went to photos and scrolled through.

There were pictures of us together. Of just her. One of me sleeping. As I scrolled, I got back to the ones she took before I'd walked into the bookstore that day. She looked happy. Carefree though I knew she'd been anything but.

She'd been trying to get away from her parents for years but when they weren't around, it looked like she was happy.

There were a few of her with a much taller blonde but all I could see was her.

The urge to slam the phone into the wall, shattering it into a million pieces hit me hard. Too many hours had passed. Too many miles had been put between us. Because if it was more than one mile, it was too much.

I fucking missed her already.

Instead of trying to fall asleep, I stared at the ceiling but the emotional toll of the day was wearing on me.

Then I heard it.

Miller. Please help me.

It was her damned voice but I couldn't tell if I'd made it up or if it was her.

I was going crazy. Hearing voices of my missing girlfriend. If I told anyone they'd think I was cracked.

But the sound of her voice jolted me with adrenaline causing my heart to race and I wasn't going to stop until I had her back in my arms.

No matter what it took.

7

HAZEL

IT HAD BEEN three days since I'd seen Miller. Three days of this place.

Caleb would come to the cabin and take the four of us to these... trainings, for lack of a better word. It wasn't like the ones that Miller had with me.

They weren't teaching us about our magic. I was assured that it would come later but I didn't want to learn it from them.

No, this was more like they were trying to sell us a timeshare. They talked about the good the coven did but as far as I could tell there was nothing good there. They spoke of our families and how we should want to keep it together.

Great news. I hated my parents. At first, I'd just wanted away from them. Now, they brought me here so now it was a full-blown hate. On the second day, it was scare tactics. The things that would go wrong if we didn't choose to declare ourselves as dark witches who belong to this shadow coven.

That was the most surprising thing and I didn't even know if Miller was aware. This shadow coven wasn't the only one. Or at least not the only branch. It made sense given that Miller's coven wasn't the only light coven but I was still taken by surprise to hear it.

"Did you hear that the girls two cabins over pledged themselves?" Nellie asked as we got ready in our own cabin to go to the next training. Today was supposed to be about the dark magic and I had a feeling that this is when my guard needed to be up the most.

"I didn't," I told her but again, no one spoke to me except these girls and Caleb.

The four of us had tried to reach out to Miller two more times but would have no idea if it had worked or not. He hadn't shown up but it wasn't like I could give him an address.

"Yeah. The weird thing is..." Gia jumped down from her bunk. "Is that I heard this process isn't even supposed to take that long. Those girls were only here two days. Now they're dark witches."

I furrowed my brows. "I've been here three days and am no closer to not telling them all to fuck off."

Juniper snickered. "Gia and I have been here even longer and I have no pull toward them."

"I did." Gia raised her hand like this was a classroom. Nellie and I both turned to her with wide eyes. This was the first we were hearing about any of us thinking of making the pledge. "Before you got here. I'd already been here a week. Was almost ready to do it. Make my parents proud for the first time in my life."

"And now?" Juniper looped an arm through hers.

Gia shook her head. "It's gone. I have zero desire to work with them. I just know that they're up to no good and all of this is smoke and mirrors."

I'd only been here a little while but hadn't heard of anyone having a change of heart. Which brought me to my next question. "What do they do with us if we don't join?"

None of them knew and as if on cue, there was a knock at the door. Caleb was the only person to come to our door which meant it was time for us to go.

The four of us shuffled out and allowed him to lead us to our next training.

"I have a question, Caleb." I glanced at the girls

quickly to see if any of them disagreed with what I was about to do.

"What's that?"

"What do they do with us if we don't join the shadow coven?"

Caleb sighed then scratched the back of his head like I made him uncomfortable. "We don't usually have that issue."

"But what if you did?"

He stopped suddenly then turned to us. "I don't think you want to know, Hazel." The serious look on his face told me that I probably didn't. At this point, I needed to.

I hadn't forgotten the lie I'd told my parents. That I'd cooperate. I just didn't care about it.

"Nothing good," he finally said.

I snapped back. "Will they kill us?"

He shook his head. "That wouldn't serve the purpose now would it?"

"I guess not," I mumbled.

"Look." He stepped closer to the four of us and Nellie's hand slipped into mine as if she wanted us to provide a united front. "The coven has been known to do shady shit to get people to follow them. I don't want that to happen to any of you so just do it." He snapped back with a look on his face that said he was surprised he'd told us this.

"What kind of shady shit?" Gia asked but Caleb shook his head and began walking again.

Late last night the four of us had hatched a plan. I was going to keep Caleb busy tonight so that Gia could sneak off to the main office to see what she could find. She basically had a photographic memory so it made sense for it to be her. Juniper was going to act as a lookout and Nellie was going to stay in the cabin to explain our absence should anyone come asking.

No one should. I'd have Caleb with me and he was the only one that came to the cabin.

We waited until the moon was high in the sky so that Gia and Juniper would have the cover of darkness. We'd tried casting a few spells to make this easier but whatever wards protected the compound must mute our powers. Or it was the damn tacker itching up my arm.

I walked as if I didn't have a purpose. Getting exercise was allowed. Actually, we were allowed pretty much anywhere at any time except the main building. We weren't allowed in there at all. So it wasn't like we were prisoners to our cabin.

Orchestrating an *accidental* run-in with Caleb

was getting easier. I'd been doing it each night as we prepared for this kind of thing. If he wasn't a shadow coven soldier I'd think we were becoming friends.

"Caleb," I called out, bringing his attention to me. He'd been talking to an older man that I couldn't see very well in the night.

That man walked away as I approached but I thought it was the same one from when I was brought in. The one with the freaky genetic mutation like Miller's giving them both those icy blue eyes.

"What's up?" he asked like we were friends and it stung to know that he could be so nice yet still did shady shit for the shadow coven.

"I wanted to talk to you about the food."

He raised an eyebrow. "Food?"

"Yeah. Like I know you are all dark and shit but does the food have to taste like actual shit?"

Caleb fought a smile. "Come on." He wiggled his fingers so that I'd follow.

While I thought he'd take me to the cafeteria kitchen or something, he instead led me down a path that led away from the camp. The one that I knew would eventually lead to the back corner where the girls and I had tried to communicate with Miller telepathically.

Once we were a bit away, he shoved his hands in his pockets. "I know what you're doing."

I furrowed my brows. "Trying to improve the dietary needs of everyone being forced here?"

He shook his head. "You've been distracting me every night."

"I'm not distracting."

He turned his brown eyes that I knew without seeing would look like liquid chocolate on me. "You're very distracting," he said quietly and something inside of me tightened.

Did he mean that in a sexual way? Or a normal one? His voice was too low to just mean that I was an annoyance. While Caleb was a good looking guy, I really hoped he wasn't interested in me. I loved Miller.

I just wished I would've opened my stupid mouth and told him before all of this happened. I hadn't and now I went to bed each night praying to a God that I didn't even believe in that Miller didn't think I'd left him for the city or some other shitty thing.

I wet my lips and my breathing increased as I realized that we were suddenly in the middle of the trees at the back of the camp, too far away from anything else for anyone to hear me scream should I need to.

"I... uh... the food..."

Now he smiled. "I know you're distracting me." He came to a stop at the same clearing that the girls and I had frequented. "And I know why."

My eyes widened and my lips tried to form an excuse that wouldn't come.

"He held up a hand to calm me. "Don't freak out. I know what you four are doing. I think Gia will find something in the main building tonight."

"How did you..."

He shrugged. "I have my ways."

"Why aren't you stopping us?"

His jaw set as I watched him search for an answer. It took many moments before he came up with, "I don't know."

"What? You don't know?" How was the possible? He made a choice not to stop us and there had to be a reason.

"I don't know," he repeated. "It's the damnedest thing. Since you showed up, things seem to be changing."

I furrowed my brows. "Things what things? I haven't done anything except every single thing you've told me to do."

"I know." He said it louder than I would've liked because underneath, I still had the fear that someone was going to happen upon us. I was supposed to be a virgin. If someone saw us together they might've thought something was going on and I didn't know what would happen. The one girl we knew of was never seen again but we didn't know what happened to her.

That was enough to scare the shit out of me.

"Listen…" He let out a frustrated sigh and tossed his hands in the air. "This is all I've known. I grew up on the stories of the shit the light coven has done to try to eradicate us. Do you know how they try to eradicate us?" I wasn't about to answer that. Not only did I not know, but I wouldn't want him to think I did. "Kill us. The light coven has been out to kill us off for probably centuries. The only way to stop that is for us to be on the offensive."

"So attack them before they attack you?"

Miller never mentioned any of this and he'd been honest with me. That I was sure of. Which meant either Caleb had been lied to his entire life or Miller didn't know.

"Exactly. We need the members. That's why there's pressure on coven members to bring their children into it. After a particularly bad battle over twenty years ago, we were almost decimated. Luckily we had a baby boom, that's when I was born. Otherwise who knows where we'd be today." He stepped closer. "But this is all I know. All I've ever known."

"OK," I said quietly, unsure as to why he was telling me all of this.

"But since you arrived and I've had to guide you… I've begun to question things. Things I shouldn't be questioning." Another step closer. "Things that are dangerous for me to question."

My heart kicked up like it was readying itself for the flight portion of flight or fight. It wouldn't matter. I had nowhere to go.

"So you're going to let us do whatever you think we're trying to do?"

Caleb snorted. "Hazel. You're trying to find out information on the coven and trying to find a way out. First, I'd like that information so that I can put all these questions to rest because right now… the way my mind is out of sorts… I don't want to be here anymore than you do." He quickly wet his lips. "Second, I already know you're not going to get out of here."

"This is kidnapping. You know that right?" Wiping my suddenly sweaty palms down my shorts might've looked dumb but I wasn't sure what was happening right now.

"Your parents wanted you here."

"I'm nineteen. A legal adult," I countered.

Caleb finally took a step back which allowed me to release some, not all, of the tension that had formed the closer he got. "There's nothing I can do about that, Hazel." His brown eyes darkened as he watched me long enough to make me squirm. "Maybe it's selfish."

"How? You didn't even know me before I got here."

He shook his head. "It doesn't matter. I like you Hazel. Maybe if you pledge yourself to dark magic, you and I could try to be together."

I bit my lips together. My instinct told me to tell him about Miller but if I did that they might assume I'm not a virgin. I'm not. But it seems that my fake purity was keeping me safe for now. It felt like a betrayal to the fact that Miller loved me and I loved him.

Deep down I knew that he'd want me to do whatever necessary to ensure that I was safe.

He just needed to hurry and figure this out.

When I didn't say anything, Caleb turned on his heel and headed back toward the cabins, probably assuming that I'd follow. I would because I had exactly zero desire to be caught out here alone. At least Caleb cared whether I lived or died and I might've been able to use that to my advantage.

"You and your cabinmates are a thorn in my side, you know that?" he asked when we were almost back to my cabin.

"And why is that?" We came to a stop in front of mine.

He scratched at his jaw. "You four should be desperate to make the pledge yet you're not. And I can't figure out why."

"Does it reflect badly on you that we aren't."

His eyes hardened and I no longer needed him to answer the question.

If he didn't come through on us, then something bad was going to happen.

"I've never had this happen before."

"Well, I don't know what to tell you." Then something else occurred to me. "Have you all been putting something in our food? Is that why it tastes like ass?"

He snorted. "I don't think I want to know how you know what ass tastes like."

A plume of fire could've come out of the ground

and swallowed me whole and I would've been grateful. What a stupid way to put it.

"But I can't tell you what we've tried with you." He took a step closer and brushed a lock of my hair off my shoulder. "Just know it's not working and it's my job to figure out why."

Then he shoved his hands in his pockets and walked away from me.

The sound from inside the cabin told me that Gia and Juniper were back. Their hushed tones when I entered told me that they were successful in finding... something.

"So?" I asked bringing all three of their attention to me.

"How did you distract Caleb?" Nellie asked.

The flush of my cheeks was back when I said, "It wasn't as hard as I thought it'd be."

Her eyes widened. "Did you..."

"No," I practically yelled. "You know I have a boyfriend but Caleb apparently thinks that once I'm in the coven he wants to try... I don't know. Dating or something. It doesn't matter."

"Doesn't matter?" Juniper raised an eyebrow. "Caleb is pretty hot. Now he's a dark witch and that clearly has its issues but I wouldn't hate looking at that face every day."

"That's because you don't have Miller." I moved in closer to see the papers that Gia was leaning over. "Now come on. What did you find?"

"A map of the compound which could be handy. We can try to find a weak spot." She took a breath, her clear blue eyes settling on mine. "But I found a list of names. The four of us are on it. Highlighted. I don't think that means anything good."

"Caleb said we're a thorn in his side. That the four of us should be desperate to become dark witches by now." I glanced at each one of them. "But we're not."

"The one thing that concerns me is that your name has a B next to it."

"What does that mean?"

She shook her head. "I don't know. I don't think it means anything good."

8

MILLER

Torture.

That was the only way I could've described waiting for my dad and Oliver to get back. Mostly because I couldn't imagine that being waterboarded was worse than the things going through my mind as I waited.

I couldn't even touch on the subject of my dad not being my dad. Excuse me. Not being my biological father.

My mother had been drugged and raped. That was how she got me and for the life of me I couldn't imagine what could've led to her keeping me. She would've had options. She didn't have to birth and raise me. My dad really didn't have to.

There were so many questions that I'd file away until later.

Finally, the guys burst back through the front door. The night had gotten dark and I couldn't begin to guess how much time had passed.

I shoved hazel's phone in my back pocket after I launched up from the couch.

"What happened?" I asked.

Dad and Oliver looked like they'd been through something and I wanted to know what. Dad wiggled his fingers to indicate that I should follow them as he marched toward the kitchen to fill two glasses with water. After sliding one over to Oliver, they both drained half while I sat there in turmoil over what they'd found out.

"You guys are fucking killing me," I told them.

Finally, Dad took a deep breath. "The address you found is definitely shadow coven. We went there. Looked around as much as we could."

"The place was crawling with dark witches," Oliver added then took another drink.

"As far as we can tell though, it's not where Hazel is."

"That's it?" I spat. "That's what took you hours?"

"No." Dad shook his head. "We did some surveillance. Listened in on a few things. It sounds like there's a camp somewhere that they sent less than cooperative witches who still need to pledge themselves to dark magic."

"You'd say Hazel is less than cooperative, right?" Oliver asked with a smirk on his face.

I snorted. "You could say that." She'd been that way with me, especially at first. Her not wanting to be told what to do helped land her wherever she is. "Where's this camp? Can we go now?"

Oliver shook his head as Dad said, "No one said where it's located. But we followed a couple of the people and think we found... something."

"Sent it to Luken so he could see what Danna can find out." Oliver took his glass over to the sink and filled it again.

"Why are you two so out of breath if you just followed a couple of dark witches?"

"Well..." Dad glanced at him and I really didn't like the silent conversation that was happening between the two.

"We didn't just follow them," Oliver offered. "One figured out we were there. He had friends. Turned into a fight."

"You're both OK?" They didn't look like either of them were hurt in any way.

"We are." Oliver slapped my dad on the back.

"Your dad is kind of a badass. Must run in the family."

My stomach clenched and my dad's gaze locked with mine.

It couldn't run in the family. I wasn't biologically related to him. Dad's jaw clenched as he shook his head.

"Nurture over nature." One corner of his mouth turned up.

I snorted. Mostly because it was true. He might not have helped create me but I was so much like him that he might as well have.

"So, what's next?" I just wanted my girl back. Safe where she belonged.

"We have to wait to see what Danna can find with the information we sent Luken," Dad explained. "Oliver got some decent pictures. She's going to see if she can' figure out who they are. That gives us something to go on. We can scry for that location. If we get lucky…"

"Until then?" I couldn't just sit there and fucking wait. What I was feeling needed action. I needed to be doing something.

"Tonight, get some sleep." I snorted because he couldn't think that was a thing that was going to happen. "Tomorrow, we start to prepare. We've got to make any potions that we think we might need. You three don't need to brush up on spells or anything but you need to make Hazel a new protection amulet that's much stronger this time."

"Stronger?" I practically yelled. "How the fuck am I supposed to make it stronger? I thought I made it as strong as I could."

Dad was nodding his understanding. "I'm going to reach out to Serena Good in the morning to figure out just how to do that. Until then, all we can do is wait."

Which was what I did.

Against everything that my body was telling me to do, I fucking waited.

That night, I fell asleep out of sheer exhaustion only to wake to voices in the kitchen.

Dad, Oliver, and Luken were standing around the island. Mom was sitting sipping her coffee looking like she hadn't been awake long. All of their eyes tracked me as I shuffled over to the coffee pot to pour a cup. But their conversation didn't stop.

There were a couple of maps spread over the island but from my vantage point, I couldn't see what they were of. My guess was wherever they thought Hazel was being held.

"Danna's on her way," Luken told me as he watched me like I was a caged animal.

Felt like I was.

"She sent a text this morning. Found some things that may or may not help." He shuffled over pulling the one map with him. "But right here, this is a dark coven meeting house. We think if we go there, we might be able to get some information."

"Let me grab my shoes." I pushed off and didn't make it two steps before Dad said, "Wait. You're going to shower and get something to eat."

"I don't-"

"You're not going to do anyone any good if you don't take care of yourself. If you collapse from lack of food when it's time to rescue Hazel, you'll be no good."

"We have to wait for Danna anyway," Luken told me more quietly.

Fine. Whatever. I hurried up to my apartment, a place I couldn't fucking stand to be right now given that my bed was still a crumpled mess from the last time I'd been in it with her. Ignoring all of that, I hopped in the shower, put on new clothes, tied my boots, and headed back in.

Mom had scrambled eggs and toast waiting for

me when I got there and had set out some pastries. I'd eat them but I couldn't taste anything.

The guys were discussing all of the possibilities of what we might encounter at the meeting house when someone knocked on the front door. Luken rushed out then came back with Danna. She had her hair pulled back and looked like she hadn't slept in days with her tired eyes drooping.

"What'd you find?" I asked without greeting.

"Well." She pulled her phone out of her pocket. "I took pictures because it was less risky than trying to take the old records." She swallowed hard. "It looks like the shadow coven has been getting more and more desperate."

"No shit."

"Which leads the council to believe that they're trying to plan for something big. None of us know why." Her eyes met mine. "We don't know why they might've taken Hazel other than her parents are more important to the coven than we thought." She turned her phone to me. "These are transfers that we know of. Hazel's parents have been giving money to the coven for years. Almost like a tithe."

"We don't do that," I countered.

"Right. But we are of the light, Miller. Who knows what crazy shit dark magic makes them do."

When I cringed she muttered, "Sorry." Then she slid her finger over the phone to another picture. "This was taken a couple of years ago and buried in the basement. I don't know why."

She turned the phone toward me to show me a man in front of a high fence that made it look like a prison camp.

"What is this?" I asked.

She shook her head. "I don't know but one of the other council members thinks it's where dark witches go to make their pledge."

"Which member?" Luken asked.

"I'm not going to tell you that. This person is risking everything by talking to me. But that member remembers one of our witches being friends with Hazel's parents. And remembers them trying to get the friend to go dark. When our witch refused, Serena had to take her into hiding."

"She still alive?" Dad asked.

Danna nodded. "She is and I was able to figure out where."

"Is it Michael?" I asked to which Danna raised an eyebrow. "Is he the one helping you that you don't want to tell us about?"

Her jaw set like concrete. "No." Her teeth were clenched together so tightly that I was surprised the word came out. "He wouldn't help me and I'm pretty sure if he knew I was helping you, you'd never see me again."

Dad furrowed his brows. "What?"

After wetting her lips, she leaned in as if she was worried someone else would hear her. "You guys know I've had some suspicions about him for a bit. Well, I'm pretty sure he's the one hiding all of this shit in files in the basement. I don't even know what I'd find if I really had some time down there."

"That doesn't make sense." Dad sounded as confused as he could be. "Michael has always protected witches of this coven."

Danna took a deep calming breath. "That's the thing. I don't think he has." She swallowed hard. "I'm only going to say this here and I can't prove it to you yet but I think Michael is a shadow coven plant. We all need to be very careful around him."

"He's been here twenty years."

"I know." She shrugged her shoulders. "I don't know why the long game... just I promise you some of the things I've seen... there's no other explanation. But I'm going to keep digging."

Luken reached out and put his hand on Danna's shoulder. "Don't do anything that puts you in danger."

Her cheeks pinked but she said, "Too late for that. I'm all in now."

Danna left after that as the five of us contemplated what to do. We all went back and forth with ideas but none sounded the best.

"You have to split up," Mom finally spoke over the noise in the room. Once she had our attention she continued. "You have to split up. Oliver and Luken, you need to go check out the meeting house. See if you can find anything. Maybe grab one of those bastards and make them talk."

The guys looked over at me while fighting a smile. My mom was basically telling them to torture a dark witch to help me find Hazel.

Fuck it. I agreed with her.

"Then Cooper, you and Miller go find this witch that had to go into hiding. If anyone is going to know what's going on with Hazel or her parents or why, it'll be here. Then everyone come back here."

Dad stepped over to mom. "I don't want to leave you alone."

"I'm fine," she insisted. "I'll add some wards to the house and work on the things you all are going to need when you go get Hazel." Her tired eyes met mine. "I'll even make sure to get her amulet charged and add every spell I can think of so that when you slip it back on her neck, she'll be protected."

After crossing the room, I wrapped Mom into a big hug. Somehow, she knew what Hazel meant to me and wasn't going to stop until I had her back.

Fuck. I said somehow but who knows what Mom saw with her psychometry in my apartment.

The four of us got ready to go do exactly as Mom directed.

Dad and I slid behind the wheel of his truck and headed out to find the witch that had to be hidden due to Hazel's parents. The crazy thing was, she wasn't that far away. At least the address Danna had given us wasn't that far away.

"What's the story with Danna and Luken?" Dad asked as we sped down the highway.

At night, in Michigan, most people kept their eyes out for deer. Well, it was daylight and I was scanning the area for dark witches.

"I don't know," I told him. When he began to protest, I said, "I really don't know. Something happened between them but he would never tell us."

"Are they together?"

"No." I shook my head. Luken didn't really have girlfriends so I didn't know what his weird relationship with Danna was.

"Tell me what happened," I said quietly and knew he'd understand what I was talking about. His hand tightened on the steering wheel.

"I don't-"

"Dad. I think I should get to know."

He worked the muscle in his haw back and forth before giving me a nod. "I don't know everything. All I know is that we were at Midsommer. Your mom's parents were looking for her. No one had seen her in a while so I started to look for her too." His hand hit the steering wheel twice. "I'd been keeping my eye on her and have no idea how I didn't notice that she wasn't there." He cleared his throat. Clearly, Dad still carried some guilt about what happened all those years ago. "We were calling for her when suddenly she was there. She'd been asleep in a field. We thought anyway."

"But she wasn't asleep?"

"No. She had no memory of anything that had happened." He cleared his throat again. "Her clothes weren't disturbed in any way... it just... it looked like she'd had too much fun at her first Midsommer."

"Until she found out she was pregnant."

Dad nodded. "She was freaking out. I told her I wasn't going anywhere."

"Here's what I don't get." I turned in my seat so

that I was more toward him. "If you two were already together, how do you know that you're not..." I let that thought linger out in the air.

I didn't yet want to say the words that he wasn't my father because as far as I was concerned he was.

"We weren't together. That didn't happen until later."

I furrowed my brows. "But you were there when I was born, right?"

Dad glanced at me then back to the road. "Yes. By then, we were together. I took her to a cabin to protect her. To protect you. If was just the two of us for months with not a lot to do but—"

"OK. I get it." I cut him off because if he was about to start talking about sex, I didn't want to hear it. Nobody did.

"I was going to say nothing to do but talk." He slapped the back of my head. "Get your mind out of the gutter. Just because we weren't together didn't mean that I wasn't already in love with her. It's just... we were friends. I don't know. It's hard to make sense of." Her turned the car sharply to the right. "Besides. We're here."

The car came to a stop in front of a modest, unassuming house. Not a single witch would've thought there was anything weird about it.

The two of us climbed out of the car and headed for the door. A mid-forties woman with short blonde hair answered, asking if there was anything she could do for us.

"I'm Cooper Campbell. This is my son Miller." He indicated me next to him. "We need to talk to you about some old friends of yours. The Riley."

The woman nodded slowly. "Serena said someone would come one day. Come on in."

As we crossed the threshold, this electric zapping covered my body. Almost like a thousand tiny fingers full of static electricity tickled my body. Once we were inside, the woman sighed.

"That ward has been there for decades," she said. "Now I know you really are from Serena's coven, I'll tell you anything you want to know." She took a deep breath. "But first tell me, is Hazel all right?"

9

HAZEL

THERE WAS a B next to my name and none of us had any idea what it meant.

It could've been nothing, I suppose, but given where I was, I didn't think it was likely. Now, how would I ask Caleb without asking him?

There wasn't enough time to figure it out of even talk about it much before there was a knock at our door. Only one person would've been knocking.

Caleb stood on the outside, never entering, I guessed because we were all supposed to be pure and having a man in our room wouldn't look good. I didn't know. Figuring out this coven when I barely knew anything about any coven wasn't the easiest thing to do.

"What can we do for you?" Nellie asked while

the three of us waited. It could've been anything. Over the last three days, we'd been taken to activities that were meant to show us that they weren't all that bad. Things that tried to manipulate us into wanting to be in the shadow coven.

It was working, too for a lot of the young women in the camp. Which was something it took me more than a day to notice.

Those staying at the camp right now were all young women. I'd overheard another ask why. She was told that it wasn't always that way but just how it worked out now. I didn't know about that. But I also didn't believe anything they told me.

Juniper had started to question whether belonging to a coven might be the right choice but between Nellie, Gia, and I we were able to bring her back.

It was brainwashing. I'd picked up on that right away. The powers that be made it clear that joining the coven had to be our choice but they were clearly trying to sway us. Brainwash us.

I wasn't sure why Juniper sometimes bought into what they were saying, or how Caleb had, but Nellie and I for sure hadn't for a second.

"You four are needed in the hall," he told us and as usual didn't say why.

"Why are we going there tonight?" I asked.

Caleb and I had already made the trek out into the trees like an hour ago. I assumed we'd be shutting down for the night soon which would give me another chance to sneak out to continue trying to break through the camp's wards.

"They don't tell me everything, Hazel." He took a step back and turned away from us indicating that he'd be waiting right there until we were ready.

We all still had out shoes on from our earlier escapades. Gia shoved the paperwork she'd found under her pillow before heading to the door.

Once we were all outside, Caleb led the way. When he took a sharp right that would leave us on a more secluded path, I knew we weren't going straight there. He kept moving until we were in an area that no one else was.

"What'd you find?" he asked me but I wasn't the one to find anything. If he was talking about this here, I had to assume it was a safe area.

He'd get into just as much trouble as we would for what we were doing.

"Nothing we could make sense of so quickly," I told him.

"Hazel," Gia snapped.

When my gaze locked with hers, all I saw was

fear. "Gia." I stepped closer to her and took her hands in mine. "I think we can trust him."

She glanced at him then back at me. "How do you know?" Her voice wavered.

My parents had been assholes but hers had instilled the fear of God into her.

"I don't," I answered honestly. "It's a gut feeling."

"Listen." Caleb stepped closer to our group and lowered his voice. "I've been in this coven my entire life. Yet once you four got here and were assigned to me, I've started questioning everything. I've done some bad shit in my life and would like it to have been for the right reason." He shook his head and ran a hand down his face. Now I wanted to know about his past. "If I'm being honest, I don't want any of you in this coven." He swallowed hard. "Plus, a lot of bad will happen if anyone finds out. But for me..." He shook his head.

"See?" I asked her. "He's in danger too."

Gia looked Caleb over before she silently nodded.

"Gia found a list with girl's names on it. We don't know what it means but we also weren't able to get through everything she brought back before you showed up."

"Did you see anything so far? Like what the fucking plan it?"

"Wouldn't you know the plan?" Juniper snapped.

Caleb wet his lips quickly. "All I know is that our numbers have been dwindling for a while."

"Imagine that," Nellie said. "People don't want to commit to dark magic."

Ignoring that, Caleb continued. "The coven has been working for decades to strengthen us. Make it a fair fight against any light coven that is a threat."

I shook my head. "See? You make it sound like the shadow coven is all about defense. But they go on the offense too right?" He nodded as if it pained him to tell me that. "So, I don't get it. What's the benefit of being dark instead of light?"

Caleb sighed. "There's a freedom in dark magic that you don't get in light magic. No worries about being good."

"I have a question." Juniper held her hand up like we were in class. "Why didn't the four of us just join a light coven. We would've been safe, right?"

Again, Caleb shook his head. "You wouldn't be able to be brainwashed by dark magic but you can switch. It's a choice you make."

"Why didn't we make the choice?" This time it

was Nellie asking the question we were all probably thinking.

"You're bound." He said this as if we all knew what he was talking about. When none of us said anything he sighed again. "Your parents have your magic bound."

"I can do magic." His dark eyes met mine like he didn't understand why I'd said that. "I can't do it well, but I was learning before I was kidnapped."

"Yeah. You can learn magic even if you're bound. But your natural ability isn't accessible. See, anyone can learn magic. Technically a human could learn it. It just wouldn't work for them the way it does us. But each witch is born with certain abilities and those can't be reached if you're bound."

"Does that mean I could be a super strong witch?" Nellie asked. "But my bitch ass parents bound it so that I can't access it?"

He nodded. "You are all strong witches. That's why you're here. Something about your natural gifts is something the coven wants." He groaned. "I can't believe I just told you all that." He stepped closer again. "Listen, I'm trusting you all here. They'd have my ass if they knew I was telling you this shit or that I was questioning... well everything."

I set my hand on his arm. Caleb glanced down at it then locked gazes with me. "You can trust us."

He waved his fingers to indicate that we had to get moving. Back on the main trail, Gia asked, "Do you know what a B next to someone's name on the list would mean?"

Caleb stopped abruptly almost causing all four of us to slam into his back. He turned slowly and put his hands on his hips. "What? Whose name has a B next to it?"

"Mine does," I told him quietly.

So many things crossed his face but his jaw clenched tightly which didn't leave me with the best feeling. "You're going to have to get out of here."

My eyes widened. "What's it mean, Caleb."

"I don't know." Yet I could tell he was lying. His reaction spoke for itself. "But we're going to have to get you out of here."

"Caleb, what does it mean?"

We stood in a stare down which meant he wasn't going to tell me. Fine. He didn't want to tell me? Then he'd do something else for me.

"Can you get a message to someone? He'll come and get me out. You won't have to risk anything."

It took him several tense moments to answer. "I

can try. If it's a light witch, it could be tricky. They might try to kill my ass before I get to them."

"It's a light witch in Echo Valley. You'll have to add where we are thought because I don't know."

"Let's go back to your cabin. I'll do it tonight."

The four of us hurried back to the cabin where I wrote a quick note to Miller then handed it to Caleb. He didn't look at it and instead folded it a second time and slid it into his back pocket. I started to tell him Miller's address but he held up a hand.

"If this witch is important to you, I don't want to know his address. I don't want to go to his house. I'll get it to him. Don't worry."

Then we had to head back out to the main hall where we had originally been wanted. It'd taken a lot longer than it should've due to our conversation and running back to the cabin.

Once we were settled in seats in the room, I watched as Caleb went over to another younger man that I'd see around here but didn't know the name of. He said something to the guy quietly, glanced back at me, and then left.

I hoped he was going to Miller.

The man standing at the front of the room, the one we were supposed to be hearing tonight, cleared his throat.

I only knew him as the director of the camp, though they didn't call it a camp. I did. There was no other way to describe where we were. Someone had referred to it as the compound, but camp sounded better to me.

He was tall, graying hair and disturbingly blue eyes. Bluer than Miller's though not dissimilar. Genetic mutation, he'd been told. It happened with some witches and had to do with the power they possessed but to me it just looked like generics.

Though neither of Miller's parents had that color eyes, so what did I know?

"Ladies, I've brought you here tonight because you've shown excellent progress."

I glanced at Nellie. The four of us had made no progress though we did pretend to just so we didn't disappear.

"Which brings me to some exciting news." He folded his hands in front of him. "We will have the pledging ceremony tomorrow night under the full moon. Each of you will commit yourself to dark magic then pledge your fealty to our coven. You will be loved. You will be protected once you do this."

An excited round of whispers carried through our group. There were probably twenty young women in this room, the four of us included. Something inside of me, a tickle of a fear maybe, once again wondered why there were no men here. Other than ones that were already coven members.

Yet there were only women.

Suddenly every warning I'd ever had about human trafficking raced through my head.

Was that the plan?

Get us nice and dark then ship us off to some old man who's high up in the shadow coven? Breed us like animals?

I hoped neither of those were true and when I thought about it, knew it couldn't be the case.

Caleb wouldn't let that happen, would he?

Then again, he'd only started to question the actions of his coven. What didn't he know?

"We will have gowns delivered to your cabins for the ceremony." He took a breath, though I'd missed most of what he said. "We look forward to tomorrow night."

The directors gazed fell on me like he already knew me. The corners of his mouth turned up like he knew a secret that I didn't when clearly, he knew all of them. Under his heavy gaze, I refused to squirm. I'd been playing along with this brain-washing as had the rest of us in the cabin but I wasn't pledging shit tomorrow night.

"Well, that wasn't creepy," Nellie said once the director was gone and we stood.

"No kidding. We better not talk about it here though," I told her.

The man Caleb had spoken to approached us which put each of us on guard. "Caleb had to step out. I'll escort you back to your cabin."

None of us said anything but instead followed the man out. There was another group of four with us, I'd guess his charges, but the two groups couldn't have been different.

My cabinmates were quiet. Tension and fear dripping from all of us. The other cabin was all a titter with excitement over being able to finally become members of the shadow coven. The brainwashing worked on them and that worried me.

Once we were back in our cabin, Nellie let go of a full body shiver. "Does that guy creep anyone else out?"

"Which guy?" Gia asked.

"The director. It's like he can see into your fucking soul."

She wasn't wrong. "Miller told me that some witches can put themselves in other's minds. Maybe that's what he was doing."

"I hope not," she countered. "He'd know that the four of us aren't drinking the Kool aid."

"I think I'm going to," Juniper said quietly.

Gia grabbed her write and gave a hard tug. "No. You're not."

Juniper turned to Gia. "I'm thinking I will."

"Why?" Gian and Juniper had been friends for a really long time. That was what long chats in the night got you. Information. "Why would you do that? Have they gotten to you?"

"No." Juniper shook her head. "I don't believe the shit they're saying but what happens if I don't?"

"What do you mean?" I asked.

"If I don't pledge tomorrow? What happens? Do I just disappear like the girl they found out wasn't a virgin?"

Fuck. I forgot about the whole virgin thing. "Wait, can you not pledge if you're a virgin?"

"No." Nellie shook her head and went over to the dresser for pajamas. "It's not that you need to be a virgin to pledge. I overheard some talk in the main building when I first got here. The virgin part is for after you pledge. Like they want to make sure no one's bringing a light fetus in here or something like that."

I let out a breath. There was no baby but I definitely wasn't a virgin.

Turning back to Juniper, I said, "Juniper, if you pledge, we can't take you with us when we leave."

"What about my family?" Her eyes filled with tears. "They might be dark witches but they've always treated me well. My family loves me and I know not everyone can relate but am I really going to go my whole life with my family being my enemy?"

She was right. That wasn't something I could relate to. Being on the opposite side of my family had almost been my plan from the beginning.

Nellie wrapped an arm around Juniper and brought her in close. "You'll have us. Listen, we can't stop you. But know that if you pledge yourself to the darkness, then dark you will be. I heard that the shadow coven once drugged a bunch of girls so they could get them pregnant. Just to bolster their numbers. Caleb said he's done a lot of bad shit." Nellie hugged her tighter. "That's not you Juniper. You're good. You'll come with us."

"To where?" she cried.

"Echo Valley," I answered without having to think about it. "There's a light coven there. They will protect you."

And I hoped with all that I was that I hadn't just lied to Juniper. I had to think the light coven would protect all of us and maybe help us get unbound.

If nothing else, we could hopefully pledge ourselves to the light which would make it harder for the darkness to creep in. Not impossible.

But at least I'd be back with Miller.

10

MILLER

W E   S T O O D near the door of the woman who was supposed to have information about Hazel's parents, waiting for her to say something. Anything. A tiny detail that would help lead us to wherever they were holding the woman that I loved.

"It's been a long time since anyone has asked about the Riley's." Carina moved further into her house but I wasn't sure I wanted to follow. Anything could be a trap but given the fact that she had a ward that I'd never heard of before made me think that wouldn't be the case.

Carina wouldn't give us her last name and no one else had either. She had to be around my dad's age but looked far closer to mine. There was something off putting about her. Something that my instincts told me to stay away from yet I was standing in her living room.

I just wouldn't get too comfortable and be on alert.

"It's important," Dad told her. "We're looking for their daughter Hazel."

"I'm sure they know where she is."

I ground my teeth together. "I'm sure they do but we can't find them either. Someone took Hazel in broad daylight. She wouldn't have wanted to go with whoever that was and I think she's in danger."

She shuffled forward as she narrowed her eyes on me. "Has she pledge herself to the coven? Her parent's coven?"

Fire burned in the pit of my stomach at the answer I was going to have to give. "I don't know. She hadn't before she was taken. Since then..."

"That's why she was taken then." Carina sat herself in a nearby chair as if standing was too much for her. Some of the things she did made her seem like an old woman. Much older than either my dad or me. "If they hadn't convinced her to pledge then they probably took her somewhere to convince her."

I took big steps forward before Carina held up her hand. "Where?"

"I wouldn't know that. I'm not part of their coven."

My gaze snapped around to Dad. "Then we need to find a dark witch and torture the shit out of him until he tells us."

"That won't work," she said even though I hadn't been talking to her. "A Shadow Coven witch isn't going to give up their secrets."

"I'd like to try."

She chuckled quietly. "Wouldn't we all." After shifting her weight in her chair she said, "I was friends with Seraphine." I raised an eyebrow because I had no idea who the fuck that was. "Hazel's mom," she explained. "I grew up with her. Thought we were friends then she hooked up with that asshole and went all in dark magic and the shadow coven. I lost my best friend but it was worse than that."

"How?" Dad asked far more gently than I would've.

Carina raised an eyebrow. "Serena Good sent you here, right?"

"In a way."

She shook her head. "It had to be her or you wouldn't have found me." She blew out a breath. "OK. Here's the story. Seraphine and I were friends.

Once her focus became that asshole and dark magic, we started growing apart."

"You're a light witch?" I asked.

"It's more complicated than that. I'm going to trust you two. Please don't make it bite me in the ass."

"We won't." My father's promise was as binding as anything in this world. That was a face.

"I suppose it doesn't matter. My time is almost up anyway."

"Are you sick?" I asked mostly because there were some illnesses that we could help her with and it explained why she sometimes moved like she was a hundred years old.

"Not sick. Just old." She sure as hell didn't look it. "I'm only half witch. My father was a Fae so while I may look thirty years old, I'm much, much older than that. The far side of me would keep me living forever, basically, but that asshole and his dark witches made sure I can never return to the Fae realm which is required of all Fae to keep their immortality."

We'd been taught about Fae growing up. Actually, we'd been taught about all the supernatural creatures that humans didn't know about. However, for the most part, Echo Valley was a safe space where we didn't have to deal with them too much. When one popped up, we had a team to take care of it. Our policy was basically if they left us alone, we'd leave them alone.

Mom had told me that our coven had become much more isolationists once Michael rose in ranks. We used to have all kinds of things with other covens, like Midsommer Festival, that we just didn't do anymore.

"So, while I waste away here... anyway." She shook her head. "The ward on the door was forged by Serena Good and me which means we combined Fae magic and light magic. Quite the combo."

"Yeah, I've never experienced anything like that." It was an awesome tick though it made me wonder what would've happened if Dad or I had been a dark witch. Would we have disintegrated?

"Would either of you like something to drink?" she asked as she pushed herself up from the table.

"I'll take a coffee if you have it," he told her as he moved further inside.

Apparently, we were trusting her.

I followed him and in moments, each of us had a coffee in front of us, though I hadn't asked for one. It'd give me something to do with my hands.

"Why did the shadow coven make sure you

couldn't go back to the Fae realm?" Dad asked gently.

"I'd like to know how." Her gaze locked on mine. "We don't have much experience with the Fae."

"How doesn't matter in this case." She took a slow drink of her coffee. "The why is what you're looking for. I wouldn't buy into the dark magic bull-shit and that put me on the other side of my best friend. Seraphine was so sure that this was the right way when I knew it wasn't. She and that asshole struggled a lot back then."

"They weren't always rich?"

She shook her head. "No. That came with the deal they made."

"Deal?" That was my dad. He didn't know most of this stuff either but I'd be grilling him in the car to see what he had already known.

"Yeah. The asshole made a deal that ensured he'd be richer than god. It came at a high cost though because when you deal with the dark fae in the human world, it always comes at a huge cost."

I swallowed hard as if I already knew the answer to the question I had to ask. "What was the cost?"

She looked at me apologetically. "A daughter."

My heart. Fucking. Stopped.

Hazel was their only daughter. They'd made a

deal to trade her for fucking money. I pushed up from the table and paced, trying to release some of the energy that had me wanting to punch this poor woman's wall.

"A daughter?" Dad asked as he watched me.

She nodded. "I don't know every detail but Seraphine told me that the cost was the betrothal of a daughter to the dark Fae. He would be able to siphon off her for decades making him more powerful than he was. So the Riley's got the money. The dark fae would get his power source."

"Siphon off?" I yelled. "What the fuck does that mean?"

"You felt the magic coming through the door. You have experienced a tiny piece of what could be if a Fae and a witch combine power. He'd be unstoppable or mostly unstoppable."

"So he'd what?" I threw my hands in the air, still pacing. "Suck her power?"

She nodded. "Little by little. The daughter was supposed to be like a battery that he could recharge from but since he was dark, she needs to be dark. It's the way it works the best. Kind of like a blood transfusion. You need the right kind."

"And they agreed to it?" Dad asked.

"They did. Asshole did pretty quickly. Seraphine took a little longer but since she'd been told years ago that children weren't possible, she didn't see the harm. She thought the debt would never have to be paid."

"Fuck!" I yelled loudly not surprising either of them. "So it's the power?"

She took a deep breath and blew it out. "The power and whatever other pleasures he wanted to take."

I stopped moving. Other pleasures? We all knew what that fucking meant.

"If she couldn't have children," Dad started. "How did Hazel come along?"

"Dark magic. They created a spell that would make her fertile against her own body's wishes. Though it was still fifty-fifty whether it'd be a girl or not."

Silence hung in the air between the three of us.

This was why Hazel's parents were so desperate for her to become a dark witch. The needed her to.

"What happens if they don't pay the debt?" I asked quietly because I wasn't giving up until Hazel was back in my arms.

"They die. It's always that they die. But it won't be quick. It won't be pretty."

"I don't fucking care. They deserve a slow fucking death."

"I won't argue with you." She took another drink then we were back to silence. I wasn't sure there was more we needed. "I wish I could tell you where they have her. My Fae magic is fading. I barely have enough to keep the wards up. If I had more, maybe I could help you find her but—"

"The information is more than enough," Dad assured her by patting her hand.

"How did they keep you from returning to your realm?" I asked.

She sighed. "They sheered my ears and marked me with the darkness. I'm not dark but I have it all around me. The doors won't open for me because of it."

"I'd still like to know why."

She looked at me so long that I wasn't sure she was going to answer. Finally she gave a little nod and said, "Because when Hazel was born, I pushed some fae magic into her. To make her more resistant to the call of dark magic. I basically marked her so they'd have a much harder time getting her into their coven. Which means a harder time paying their debt. It doesn't last long and she could always choose on her own but then they bound her natural powers which the Fae magic had attached itself to. So..."

She didn't know what that meant or how it'd work. I understood.

But Hazel had been protected at least a little bit with the Fae magic even if that magic was now fading. She'd had it and I had to hope she still did a little.

Dad had told me about binding before. Some witches did it with their kids until they're old enough to understand. Now I was thinking that sometimes they bound the powers for their own selfish fucking reasons.

Binding Hazel's natural magic put her at risk and if I could get my hands on her parents, I wouldn't need magic to rip them apart.

Before I could ask anything else, my phone rang and I couldn't ignore it. No one was going to be calling me to catch up right now because everyone I knew also knew what was going on. The entire coven knew.

"I have to answer this," I told them then took the three steps into the kitchen before accepting the call. "Hello?" I already knew it was Luken and was hoping with everything I had that he'd found something.

"Hey. You still at the witch's house?"

"Yeah." I'd tell them all everything but not here where she could possibly hear me. "Did you find anything?"

"Nothing important," he said but sounded slightly out of breath. "Maybe a few clues but that's not why I'm calling. We need you and your dad here now. Like as quickly as that car can carry you."

Fear, dread, and hope all pooling in my stomach like a sick potion made as a Halloween prank. "Why?"

"Danna got a message from Hazel."

Relief washed over me. I didn't even know the details but at least I knew she was still her. "What's it say? How?"

"Just get back here man. Oliver and I will start getting shit together to go get her. But you've got to hurry."

I ended the call without saying goodbye then hurried out to my dad. He and Carina were mid conversation when I said, "We have to go now." Dad furrowed his brows. "That was Luken. Danna got a message from Hazel."

Dad was on his feet, thanking Carina for her time then both of us were headed for the door.

"Wait!" Carina was moving to a side cabinet.

When she turned she had a small drawstring bag in her hand. She pulled it open so that we could see maybe six small potion bottles. "Take it."

"What—"

"It's my blood," she explained. "From back when my Fae magic was far stronger. It's all I have left and I think you're going to need some help."

"If we take that," Dad says then you won't be able to charge your wards the way you're supposed to." How he knew that, I had no idea.

Carina shook her head. "My time is almost done anyway. I don't care at this point and if I can help Hazel Riley, that's what I want to do."

Dad nodded, went to her and took the satchel then he and I were in the car heading back to Echo Valley.

He pushed the car as hard as he could, the speedometer getting lost somewhere to the right where it dropped off into an abyss while I kept muttering the blurring spell I'd learned in middle school that would hopefully mean a cop wouldn't see us and try to pull us over. We wouldn't stop. That much I was sure of.

The car hadn't come to a full stop outside my parents' house before I flung myself out and raced up the stairs with Dad right behind me.

"What is it?" I asked as soon as I got through the door. "Where is it?"

Luken walked over and handed me a piece of paper. Mom, Danna, Luken, and Oliver waited as I opened it.

It was a quick note. Almost nothing. She was with the shadow coven, which we knew. They were trying to brainwash her into pledging and the pledging would be tomorrow night. She wasn't going to do it and didn't know what would happen if she didn't. Though she might pledge just to protect everyone. She didn't know where she was but it was a camp of some sort.

And she loves me. Very much.

Fucking hell. I fell to my knees holding that note. It was her writing. There was no question about that. I'd learned what that looked like in fucking middle school.

"Make sure to look at the bottom," Luken said quietly.

In a different script, someone wrote down an address not too far from Echo valley.

"That has to be the camp, right?" I looked up at him as I tried to handle my emotions.

Hazel probably didn't even know what was in store for her if she makes that pledge and joins the coven. If she did, I hoped she wouldn't even consider making it no matter what she thought was protecting everyone.

"Looks like it," Luken told me. "If she says she might do it to protect everyone then that has to man the shadow coven is using you to get to her. She wouldn't want anything to happen to you."

"Fuck that." I pushed back up to my feet and handed the note to Dad but was going to want it back. "How'd you get it?" That was for Danna.

"I was unlocking my apartment when a man approached me." She ran a hand up her arm. "He held his hands up and said that he comes in peace. That he has a message from Hazel Riley. Then he handed it to me and put some distance between us probably because he knew I was about to fry his ass." Danna had a knack for calling electricity with the snap of her fingers. "Anyway, he said it was all there. To get her out before tomorrow night and that he'd do what he could. Then he was gone."

"You didn't stop him?" I march toward her until Luken slid in front of me, stopping me from doing something stupid.

"No, I didn't stop him," she snapped. "Why would I? I don't want some dark witch around me."

"We could've—"

"We have what we need," Luken cut me off. "Now, let's get our shit together and make this happen."

He was right.

I wasn't going to get lost in the details because this was my fucking chance to get Hazel back.

And I wasn't going to waste it.

11

HAZEL

"WHAT THE FUCK IS THIS?" Nellie stood with one hand on her hip and the other on the doorknob.

Caleb was on the other side holding four garment bags in his hand. "It's what you're required to wear tonight."

She furrowed her brows then glanced back at me. "Required to wear?" I thought she was asking him but she was looking at me the entire time.

"Yeah." He sighed. "It's part of the ceremony. It will take place in the clearing under the moon."

"What if it's cloudy?" Gia asked. "If we don't have the moonlight would it be canceled?"

He shook his head, I thought because he was quickly becoming used to us. He probably thought

Gia was going to try to create clouds. Wait. Was that something witches could do?

"No," he told her. "It wouldn't be canceled. You still get moonlight through the clouds."

"Come in here," I whispered loud enough for him to hear."

"It's against the rules, Hazel."

I dropped my shoulders. Yes, it was against the rules but who would know? And why was it against the rules? Oh. Right. Some dumb thing about those of us here at least today being pure. I hadn't even had time to process the fact that my parents knew so little about me that they thought I was still pure.

After moving closer to the door, I asked, "Who would know? I don't want anyone to overhear me."

Caleb glanced around quickly then took a step inside far enough that Nellie could close the door then he moved to an area that you wouldn't see him if you glanced in the window.

These rules were idiotic. Just because he was in this room with four supposed virgins didn't mean we'd all suddenly become his harem.

"Did you deliver the message?"

He nodded. "Not to the address you gave me. I went to one of the members of the coven's council. Took her by surprise and gave her the note."

"Did you and she fight?"

"No. I gave it to her then took some space. She has it." He shrugged. "I don't know why they haven't come for you."

"Well she has it. I don't know much about the council or the coven really but just because she has it doesn't mean she gave it to Miller."

Caleb's jaw tightened. "Are you and Miller..."

That wasn't something I wanted to answer right now. There was nothing I wanted less than to disappear like the other girl did.

"He'd come for me," was all I told him instead.

"So what are these?" Nellie was standing before us with one of the garment bags opened to a long black dress. Beautiful if under other circumstances. It had a Victorian gothic vibe to it. Long and black, it had floral lace over the bodice that went to the neck and butterfly sleeves, a thin satin belt around the waist that led to a flared soft skirt.

In any other situation, that was a dress I'd want to buy for a special occasion. In this one, I didn't want to put the thing on.

"All of us have to wear this?" I asked, not taking my eyes off the dress.

"Yes." Caleb's voice was a lot closer to me than it had been which caused me to glance over. There was a heat in his eyes that I couldn't place. I wasn't sure it was quite desire but I couldn't find a name for it. "All of you will be wearing the same one. There are names on the garment bag. They got your sizes from your parents."

Gia hurried over to join our little group. "Why are there only women here?" That was definitely meant for Caleb.

"It's not always. Just this group and no, I don't know why. There's a lot of details I'm not told."

"And you believe this is the right thing to do?" I asked quietly like he and I were the only ones in the room when clearly we weren't.

His dark eyes lingered on mine. "I used to, but now... I'm not sure. I wish this wasn't happening to you." He glanced around as if he just remembered that there were others in the room. "The four of you. I've never had any issue leading a group to the coven but with you four... I don't know. I told you I'm questioning everything and it fucking sucks."

"Sucks?" I furrowed my brows. "Why?"

He quickly wet his lips as the four of us watched him war with himself. "Sucks because I belong to something that I don't think I believe in anymore. Leaving isn't the easiest. I have no family. I'll lose all of my friends. You four will be part of the coven—"

"Ah, no. No I won't." This was a huge risk but I was going to take it. "I don't really care what happens, I'm not pledging myself to dark magic. I'm not committing to the shadow coven."

His eyes widened. "I don't think you know what that means."

"I don't think I care what it means. I can't do it."

"Your parents are going to be there," he said louder before taking a deep breath. "Do you know what they're going to do?"

I raised an eyebrow. "Do you think my parents are going to kill me? When this is so important to them? Wouldn't they just keep trying to convince me?"

"No," he snapped causing me to flinch. "You don't know what it will cost them. You don't know why this is so important."

"And you do?" I yelled. "Because if you do, tell me."

He clenched his teeth together. "I can't. It's not because I don't want to it's because I'm compelled not to."

Furrowing my brows, I took another step closer. "What does that mean? What aren't you telling me?"

"Hazel," Gia said quietly. "If he's compelled not to tell you, he really can't. He could confirm it if you guessed but I'm thinking it's not something you can guess, right?" That was for Caleb.

"Right."

"Who compelled you?" He bit his lips together and shook his head.

"He can't tell you that either," she told me. "Unless we could break the compulsion but there's no way we'd find the ingredients to do that. I read about it in a book my parents had. Since I grew up knowing about this stuff, they didn't hide shit from me. It's another level of dark magic. It's something they can do or rather the right dark witch can do but only to other dark witches. That's why our parents couldn't just compel us to join the coven."

"Every single thing I learn about the world is weirder than the last." At least those words brought a chuckle.

"Listen." Caleb moved closer to me. "I don't want this for you. I don't want you to pledge but I also don't want what happens if you don't."

The fact that he knew what would happen had my heart racing. He hadn't told me and I wasn't sure that I wanted him to. Before he'd come into the cabin I'd been resolved to not pledge no matter the cost. I couldn't do that to Miller and I couldn't do that to myself.

If I pledged, from what I could tell, that would make Miller my enemy. There's no world I could exist where that would be OK.

"I have to go." Caleb moved back to the door, cracked it open to have a look around, then slipped out quickly without another word.

Each of us took the bag with our name on it and went back over to our bunks. I hung mine on the end and stripped it open. At least whoever planned this part had taste. The dress was beautiful.

"He's got a thing for you," Nellie said quietly as if Gia and Juniper wouldn't have heard her anyway.

"Who are you talking about?" I kept my eyes on the dress to not betray the fact that I knew who she was talking to.

"Caleb."

Now I turned to her. "No, he doesn't. He doesn't want this for any of us."

She cocked her head to the side and narrowed her eyes. "You can't be that unaware. He's questioning everything because of you. He doesn't want any of this for us because of you."

After swallowing hard. "I don't think that's true."

She grinned. "OK, Hazel. If that's what you want to believe, but I think he wants you as his. Probably thinks he can have you after you pledge."

"I'm not pledging."

She rolled her eyes. "I know that and you know that but he seems to think you don't have a choice."

"Miller will come for me."

She threw her hands out in the air. "Then where the hell is he? We're kind of getting down to the wire."

"I don't know." It was something I'd thought of myself. I sent the message yesterday. He should've been here by now. "Maybe whoever Caleb gave the message to didn't believe and therefore didn't give it to him."

"Or we're just on our own."

I was already shaking my head before she finished her sentence. "No. There's a reason and I'm not giving up hope. When he gets here and gets me out you three are coming with me."

"I can't," Juniper said so quietly that I almost missed it.

"Junie, you can." Gia wrapped her arm around her best friend.

"You know that I can't." Juniper's dark eyes began to water. "I don't want to do this but I don't have a choice. I have to join the shadow coven."

"Why?" I asked. "What could possibly be so important?"

"Her brother," Gia answered for her. "But Junie, we could get him out before they do this to him."

"How?" she asked both as if she didn't believe there was a way and hoped like hell Gia had a plan. "You know that I can't leave him with my parents."

"We'll find a way," I told her. "You can't sacrifice yourself—"

"Do you have siblings?" she cut me off and I shook my head. "Then you don't know what I'm talking about. If I don't do this, I won't get to see him and he'll be left to the wolves."

"You'll be our enemy," Gia told her.

"Then I'll have to be your enemy. Listen, I'd hoped beyond hope that we'd be able to stop this but we can't. The three of you should think about that before deciding to cross the shadow coven."

Nellie moved to the middle of the circle we created. "Well, that creates a big problem for me Juniper. We've told you things. Secret things."

Tears were now falling down her face freely. "I'll never betray that confidence. Pledging myself to dark magic won't change who I am. It will change my magic and I won't ever tell anyone anything we've talked about."

"You'll spend your life doing shitty things and that will kill your spirit." Gia knew her better than we did and she knew about this stuff more than we did. She was the perfect person to handle this.

"Maybe I'll get my brother and get out."

But Gia was already shaking her head. "That's not how it works now is it?"

The two of them held their gazes on each other as if they were in a stalemate. Which they were. It didn't seem like we were going to change Juniper's mind. No, that was made up.

"I'll miss you, Juniper," I told her quietly right before the four of us went into a group hug.

Once we turned around to begin getting ready for the ceremony, Nellie whispered, "I swear, Hazel, your man better come through."

As if I wasn't thinking that myself already.

Before getting dressed, I wandered out to the clearing and let the cooler breeze calm me. I'd been doing this each day, grounding myself to the elements the way Miller had taught me. Then I cleared my head and focused on him.

It'd only been days since I saw him. Probably I shouldn't miss him as much as I did but I thought that was more the prospect of never seeing him again.

If I didn't pledge, would they really kill me? Was

there some worse fate that Caleb couldn't tell me about? I couldn't think of one other that whatever ended with me not back to Miller.

This was unforgivable. My parents had raised me for any other reason than this and the realization that they likely never even loved me was more than I wanted to think about. I had enough going on.

As I did all of those things, the memories of the last morning with Miller took over. His hands sliding over my body. His lips nipping at my skin. It was as if I could actually feel it though I was annoyed that he and I had wasted so much time. If he hadn't been such a boy I could've had him in high school but I guess this was just how it was meant to work out.

I got a glimpse of happiness. A tiny morsel of something that was just for me.

Now I was a witch who'd become a prisoner of a shadow coven that had some nefarious plan for her.

Not exactly how I thought my life would go.

As I stood there with my eyes closed, memories playing in my mind, the waning sun shining its last rays down on me, a loud crack of thunder made me jump and brought me right back to the now.

It was a clear day. Where the hell did that thunder come from?

I didn't see any signs of bad weather but still, I hurried back to the cabin to dress for the ceremony. Those moments alone were meant to clear my mind but all it did was strengthen my resolve.

No matter what threat was made against me, I wasn't joining the shadow coven. I just wasn't. Even if that put Miller in some kind of danger, I had to believe he could handle himself.

"Where have you been?" Nellie asked as soon as I came through the door.

"The clearing. I wanted a moment to myself before... well, before whatever happens, happens." I hurried over to my bed and tore my shirt over my head.

"We don't have long," Gia offered. "They'll start the ceremony before the moon is fully up then wait for us to pledge until it is."

"I'm hurrying."

Though the four of us dressed in silence, we were all thinking about Juniper and her decision to remain with her family. I wanted to fight it but it was going to be hard enough to avoid pledging myself and I couldn't ask someone to possibly face death instead of doing what she thought was right.

I'd grown close to her though so I'd miss her.

Because if I could get out of here, Nellie, Gia, and Caleb were coming with me.

The four of us stood in a tense silence when a knock came on the door. It was Caleb, no doubt, coming to take us to the ceremony.

It was time to fight for a chance to see Miller again.

12

MILLER

"Why can't we go now?"

The idea that we wouldn't leave to find Hazel immediately ate at my stomach like bad gas station sushi.

Fuck this. I didn't want to wait.

"I think we should speak with the council," Mom said. "We can't do that until morning."

It had gotten a lot later than either Dad or I realized while we were inside Carina's house. I knew that time moved differently with the Fae and she was half fae but did that mean it moved differently in her house?

I didn't think so but fuck it was late.

"I don't think we should do that," Danna countered then glanced at Luken for what looked like reassurance. Of what? No idea and also no fucking cares in the world.

All I cared about right now was getting Hazel back.

When she didn't say anything, Luken took a step forward. Danna had barely met my parents so I could understand her being uneasy sharing everything with them. However, my parents were on my side no matter what.

"Danna has suspected that the shadow coven has infiltrated our coven," he told them.

Oliver snorted. "That sounds very cloak and dagger."

We heard him but also ignored him.

"I don't think that's possible," Mom countered then looked over at Dad. "Is it?"

"I mean, technically anything is possible, right?" He folded his arms over his chest which was something I did all the time.

In moments like that, I thought it was going to take a while to sink in that he and I weren't biologically related. Some of our mannerisms were so fucking similar.

"Why do you think that?" he asked her with no doubt or accusation in his voice.

She shook her head. "It would take too long to go

through everything but it's been building for a while. I don't know who though. Not yet."

"And she's risked herself to get us information," Oliver added which was true. If the shit hit the fan, Oliver, Luken, and I would have her back. There was no doubt of that.

"It doesn't make sense." Mom shook her head as she spoke. "The council has been in place for years. You're the newest member. Everyone else has been there since Serena left more than fifteen years ago."

"Mrs. Campbell, I know it's hard." Danna came closer then reached out to take Mom's hand. "I've had to go in there every day pretending that I don't know what I know. Or what I suspect and it's absolutely possible it's more than one member. But considering that we have dark witches living in Echo Valley, I just don't think it's a stretch."

Mom took a deep breath and squeezed Danna's hand. "It's not. We knew Hazel's parents didn't' want anything to do with the coven but some witches don't. They want to be lone wolves, so speak."

I groaned. "Please don't mention wolves. That's all we need right now."

A low rumble of laughter spread amongst the group.

"You're right." Mom pulled away from Danna but

didn't go too far. "As far as we know, only the people in this room know what's happening right?" A murmur of agreement came from all of us. "So, we can't go tonight." That was for me.

"You're not going at all," Dad countered which got him a scowl from Mom.

"I agree." I couldn't have my mother anywhere near the coven that violated her. I wouldn't make her do that or even let her put herself through it even though I knew she would.

I guess there were limits to what I'd do to get Hazel back.

After a pointed look at my father, she continued. "Anyway. I agree, not tonight. I'm sorry Miller. I know it's hard not to just charge out there. But I think I have a plan."

Mom dove into how she thought this would work best. It was late, past midnight. She wanted everyone to get some sleep though I protested. There was no fucking way I was going to sleep. But she felt if we could recharge, it would help us when we headed to the camp tomorrow. Or today. What the fuck ever. She thought it best that we go when the moon is at least visible in the sky which would help us ground and power whatever we needed to take with us.

Then tomorrow, we could pack. Make extra potions. Use the far blood for what it was intended, though I didn't know what that was. Mom seemed to thought she wasn't going to get into it tonight. Some potions would be made using the Fae blood Carina had given us. Mom seemed to know what those would be and for some reason, so did Danna.

Then we could leave early enough, find this fucking camp and get in there while the moon was still rising. It'd give us enough time to harness the power of the moon for hours if necessary. No matter what went wrong.

Also, Mom promised to use her psychometry on the note to try to sketch out as much of the camp as she could see. It might've ended up being nothing or it might've ended up being something.

If we left now, we'd have limited time to get Hazel out. If we met problems or opposition, who knew. We'd be outnumbered, that was for sure so that meant waiting until every element could be on our side.

No matter how much it fucking sucked.

I hated to admit it but Mom was right.

I had to wait another night.

At Mom's insistence, we were all staying in the house with them. She couldn't handle the thought of all of us be scattered about in case the shadow coven decided to attack or if anything else went wrong.

Here, we had Mom and Dad, older, more experienced witches to back us up.

Our house had three bedrooms. Mom and dad's, my old one, and a guest room that almost never got used. When I was a kid I thought Dad had it set up in case his sister ever came home. His parents were gone now so she wouldn't have anywhere else to go.

Danna took the guest room. Oliver and Luken did rock, paper, scissors to see who'd stay in my old room after I insisted I probably wasn't going to sleep so a bed would've been wasted on me.

The couch would be fine.

Oliver won so Luken grabbed a couple of blankets and extra pillow out of the linen closet and came back downstairs where I was laying on the couch.

"You can have it," I told him.

"Nah. The floor is fine. Maybe you'll get some sleep up there."

"Doubt it." But I had taken my shoes off and pulled Hazel's phone out of my pocket again when a thought occurred to me. "Do you think her parents might track her phone?"

"Yeah probably." He laid his head back on the pillow he'd brought down.

Dad was still down here going over every window and door, making sure they were sealed and protected for the night so I knew he could hear us.

"So when we get her back..."

"Going to have to trash the phone," he said what I already knew the answer was.

I shook my head. She'd lose everything in there. As I laid on the couch, I began air dropping every picture she had on her phone. Surprisingly there weren't that many but whatever was there, I didn't want her to lose. I'd get her another phone and put them on that.

"You really love her don't you?" It was dark outside and quiet in the house. Dad moved like he was a fucking ninja and Luken's voice was the only thing breaking the silence. He spoke quiet enough that those upstairs probably couldn't hear him.

"Yeah. I fucking do." There was an edge to my voice that wasn't really directed at him but more at the situation.

He chuckled because he heard it too. "I can't believe you got her to give you the time of day given what a fucker you were to her."

Those memories brought a smile to my face. It

was a big one but it was still there. "I wasn't the only one now was I?"

"Yeah but Oliver and I were following your lead man. Did you tell her that we also kept every other guy in the school away from her?"

"I did."

Dad chuckled quietly.

"How'd she take that?"

"Not the best." All three of us laughed at that.

I knew what Luken was doing and honestly, it was part of the reason he was one of my best friends. Him and Oliver would do whatever it took to help me get Hazel back. It'd been merely days. I couldn't imagine a lifetime apart.

He didn't know about the deal her parents had made with the dark fae and that was something I was going to have to tell them tomorrow. Or I thought so anyway. Maybe they didn't need to know. But maybe knowing would make them push harder.

"We'll deal with it tomorrow," Dad said when he patted my shoulder as he passed by me.

Now all I had to do was wait the hours until it was acceptable to get up again.

Mom had been right. We all needed to sleep. I even nodded off eventually probably due to sheer exhaustion.

When my eyes popped open in the morning, I found that I'd slept far too fucking late and the guilt kicked in. Was Hazel sleeping at night? What was she dealing with?

I groaned as I pushed myself up.

Luken wasn't on the floor anymore. His blankets were folded and neatly stacked onto of the pillows and set on the nearest chair.

Voices traveled from the kitchen so that was where I was headed. Everyone was around the island with coffee and breakfast, chattering away about what we were doing today.

"Why'd you all let me sleep so late?" I poured myself a cup that would hopefully wake my ass up.

"Figured it was better than you watching the clock," Luken told me.

"Plus, you needed to sleep," Oliver added. "The rest of us have been getting some hours the last few days. I don't think you have. You need to be on your A game so we don't all die."

I grunted so he'd know I heard him and he wasn't wrong. If I'd gotten two hours a night since she was taken, I'd be surprised.

"So what's the plan?" I grabbed a slice of toast to eat as I went to join them at the island.

"Everyone's going to do what they need to for

themselves. Shower. Get clothes," Mom explained. "Then we're meeting back here. I'm going to spend some time with the note once we've cleared out. Danna is going to begin making the potions. Your dad put the Fae blood in the potion room."

"Then around seven, we're going to head out." Dad took a long drink but kept his eye on me like he was expecting me to freak out. I wanted to. Seven was so fucking far away but I'd agreed to this and was going to follow it.

Soon after, everyone went on their way. Since I had nothing better to do, I did take a shower and change my clothes. As if I needed clean clothes to fight the shadow coven but it was something that took up time.

When I got to the potion room, Danna was already there working.

"OK. So the Fae blood is mostly for us." She dropped something into the mortar then began crushing it with the pestle. "It's going into a potion we will each drink. The Fae blood will help us get past their wards. Given that the shadow coven is making deals with Fae, I doubt their wards protect against them."

"So it will trick the protection wards?"

"Yes." She dropped whatever she'd been

grinding into a small bottle, turning the liquid purple. There were four bottles.

"Four?" I asked.

"Yeah. You, Oliver, Luken, and your dad. I'm staying here with your mom." She glanced up at me then continued working. "Your dad is adamant your mom stay behind."

"I am too."

"It makes practical sense as well. She and I can make sure we're ready in case…"

"One of us gets hurt?"

"Yeah. She's a kickass healer so we'll be ready for anything."

Mom was a kick ass healer. It wasn't her natural ability. That was psychometry but it had been important to her that she be able to heal anything that crossed her path. There were some natural diseases she obviously couldn't beat but anything I'd ever hurt, she'd been able to fix.

"Hazel's a sweet girl," she said without looking at me.

"I know."

"How in the hell did you convince her that you deserved her?" A smile played on Danna's lips.

"I don't." It was an immediate answer. Hazel was a better person than me and I knew it.

Danna's hand landed on my back, the warmth going through my T-shirt onto my skin. "We've got this, Miller. She'll be back here tonight. Then we'll deal with the shadow coven." I glanced over to find her eyes dark. "All of them. We're cleaning house."

"What if you're the only one left after we do that?" I'd meant it as more of a joke but in reality it could happen.

She snorted. "Well, then I get to lord over all of you."

I chuckled and it felt good to be so close to having Hazel back.

"I've got it," Mom called from the kitchen which brought Danna and me running from potion room and the rest of them from wherever they'd been.

"You got what?" I asked as soon as I was next to her. Dad slid in on the other side.

"The camp. Or it looks like a camp. The location on the note wasn't super specific given that this probably doesn't have an actual address but here." She slid a piece of paper over.

On it, she'd drawn a rough sketch of what she'd seen. It looked like an old sleepaway camp. Probably had been at one time. Now we had a layout. The cabins were in one part, the main buildings across from it but there was an area of trees that were dotted with small clearings.

"I tried to look in every corner," she said apologetically. "But there are some blind spots. I don't know why. I tried to put into the future but that was much harder. All I kept seeing is young women in black dresses. I don't even know if it was at the camp." She glanced up at me with apologetic eyes. "I'm sorry I couldn't see more."

"No," I told her immediately. "This is perfect, Mom. It's what we need. Right?" That was directed at Dad.

"Yes. This is great, Eden. We don't need anything else. You rest up." He leaned his elbows onto the island as we all looked over the drawing. "I think we should enter the camp back here." His thick finger landed on the same spot I'd been eyeing. It was near a clearing toward the back of the camp.

"I agree," I told him. "Then we can make our way through the trees probably unnoticed." I trailed my finger to indicate where I meant. "Get to the cabins and find Hazel."

"Are we just storming the cabins?" Oliver asked. "I mean I'm happy to do it but they'll notice."

"I don't think that's a good idea." Luken thunked

him on the back three times. "No matter how much fun it might've been.

"I agree." I took moment to think about it. "First, Oliver, we need your spell. The one you used when we were last fighting those witches."

"The communication one. Yeah. I've got it." He tapped the side of his head with his index finger. "That way we can talk to each other without drawing attention."

"Exactly. Then I think we all make our way up but I'll go cabin to cabin to find her. I can be quiet." I swallowed hard, pushing down the anticipation running through me. "When I find her, I'll get her out."

"Are we taking them all?" That was Luken. I'd been so focused on Hazel that I didn't even consider the other girls at the camp."

"What do you think?" I asked Dad.

He quickly wet his lips. "I think you focus on Hazel. Sure, if others want to chance getting out, we won't deny them but if we try to take the whole camp with us... we don't know how many people that is. It'd make it harder to get away."

Which meant make it harder to get Hazel out of there.

While nodding I said, " Hazel is the priority but a

lot of those girls are going to already be ready to pledge the coven. We can't help them."

Now that we had a plan, all we had to do was pack up and head out there.

I was minutes away from having Hazel in my arms again.

And I couldn't fucking wait.

13

HAZEL

THE CEREMONY BEGAN with less pomp that I would've expected. After all, they made us dress up in these Wednesday Addams dresses and made it sound like this was going to be life changing.

Sure, for those that drank the Kool aid, it probably would've been. I started referring to it that way because there was a potion that you apparently had to drink. Or at least that was what I'd seen three girls do already. Gia leaned over to whisper that the potion was for dark magic. You didn't need it but it would held lift any bindings as well as prove this was what you wanted.

Then there was the pledge to the coven.

A small cut to the palm of your hand to make your blood sacrifice.

I'd never understood that.

Why cut the palm of your hand? It was basically the worst place to do it. Or a fingertip. That fucker you'd break back open every time you moved. Why not a small cut the arm?

I guess it looked cooler on the palm? I didn't know and wasn't about to find out.

The four of us sat there, holding each other's hands in a row while my leg bounced with nervous energy. It took me moment of scanning the people standing guard to find Caleb. Once our gazes locked, his jaw tensed.

"He looks intense," Nellie whispered so that no one else would hear her.

"Almost like this is hurting him more than us," Gia added.

Before I could respond, Nellie said, "Like you becoming a dark witch like him is the last thing he wants to see happen."

I shook my head quickly. "It's not just about me. It's about all of us."

"Yeah," Gia sort of agreed. "Though he knows what's supposed to happen to you after you pledge even if he can't tell us and he isn't happy about it."

Caleb folded his arms over his chest and shifted his weight form one foot to the other. He was wearing dark washed jeans and a black T-shit like they all were. His dark hair was a mess like he'd pushed his fingers through it more than once and his dark eyes I couldn't see but I knew they were on me.

There had to be something we could do. Some last ditch effort to not be put in this position.

It was surreal. These could've been my last moments alive because we had no idea what would happen when someone refused. No one had. I'd be the first without question. No way was Nellie or Gia going first.

Suddenly, Juniper stood. "No, Juniper," I begged, reaching out for her hand.

She looked at me with tear filled brown eyes and said, "I'm sorry. I can't leave my brother behind."

Then she took a deep breath, shook out of my grip, and marched to the alter.

Her voice didn't crack a single time as she made her pledge to the shadow coven. She'd made her decision and that was it.

No matter how much we hated it or how it broke our hearts.

Thunder cracked loudly following a glow in the sky that reminded me of heat lightning. It was dark, the moon was high and the air had cooled off. Right after a bright bolt of lightning hit the ground not far from the alter.

We all hopped to our feet. "Something's happening," I whispered while clenching Nellie and Gia's hands tightly in my own. "Maybe this is our chance."

I glanced over at Caleb again but he wasn't standing there anymore. He was running toward us. Before he could even get close, something pushed him back right before the fence near the clearing exploded into splinters.

The girls of the camp screamed together and weren't sure what to do. Nellie, Gia, and I stood there, holding onto each other because we didn't know what to do either. What I did know was that I wouldn't waste this chance. If the shadow coven's attention was diverted, I was going to take the opportunity.

"We should get out of here," I told Nellie and Gia without looking at them. Watching the mayhem that was breaking out seemed more important at the time. I scanned our surroundings trying to determine the best way to go.

Out that fence had my vote but there was a magical battle taking place complete with balls of color flying in both directions.

"What is that?" I asked while staring at the color

show.

"Magic," Gia told me right away. "Everyone's magic has a color. At least when you get good enough or unlock your natural talents. You can train yourself to do spells with the flick of your wrist but not when you're bound."

"Can we learn about this later and get the fuck out of here now?" Nellie yanked my arm. She wasn't wrong.

If the fight was happening by the fence, the best bet was to go through the camp and out the front.

"We need to go that way." I pointed back toward camp. "And get these damn trackers out as soon as possible."

They agreed and we went running. Most of the girls had already pledged so they joined the fight. Whoever came through that fence was going to be outnumbered, I had no doubt but I hoped they'd at least keep the shadow coven distracted long enough for us to get out of there.

We were running, hurrying through the trees on the path back toward camp. Every so often I'd glance back to make sure we weren't being followed.

Which was why I didn't notice anyone in front of us until I smacked into a bigger than me man like he was a brick wall causing me to lose my balance.

Shit. I should've been watching both ways.

I backed away and was about to run when he said, "Hazel. Fucking finally."

Slowly I brought my eyes up and when I found Miller gazing down at me, relief flooded my body and tears fell down my cheeks. I didn't know I could be so happy to see a person.

"Miller." I threw myself at him. He caught me of course, wrapped both arms around me and lifted me off the group. He held me tightly like he didn't want to let me go.

I didn't want him to and if I had any say about it, he wouldn't.

One arm remained wrapped around my waist while the other slid up my back until it settled on the back of my neck. Miller brought his lips down to mine.

This wasn't a kiss that we'd shared before. This was relief. Nothing else. He had found me. He'd come to me like I'd wanted him to.

When he pulled away he whispered, "I heard you. I thought I was going crazy but I heard you."

The tears wouldn't stop. At least not until I remembered that we weren't alone.

I wiggled out of his arms but he took my hand in

his like he thought if he didn't physically have a hold of me, he'd lose me again.

"This is Nellie and Gia. They're my roommates." Then I looked at them and slid closer to Miller. "This is Miller."

"The boyfriend." Gia let out a breath that showed she'd been on high alert, ready to try to take anything on. "I thought you'd never make it."

"Yeah. It wasn't easy to get here when I didn't know where here was."

"You got my message?" I asked him. His icy blue eyes looked down at me as he nodded.

"Then my mom used it to get us the layout so we could plan this." He stooped down so that we were at eye level. "I'm sorry it took me so long."

Shaking my head, I said, "It doesn't matter. You're here now."

He kissed me again quickly before standing at his full height. "Did any of you confirm the dark magic? Pledge the shadow coven?"

"No," the three of us answered at the same time.

"Our roommate Juniper did but you all came in right before I was about to go up there."

His jaw tensed. "Were you—"

"I wasn't going to do it. I did plan on telling them to go fuck themselves but then the fence blew up."

He snorted, showing the first hint of a smile on his tired face. Made me wonder what he'd been through since I was gone. In a matter of days, the entire world had turned upside down.

"Do you two want to come with us?"

Gia's eyebrows shot up. "If it gets us the hell out of here, yes."

He nodded then turned, ready to lead us out of here but he didn't get two steps before Caleb blocked our path ten feet in front of us. His arms were folded over his chest like he didn't have a care in the world or wasn't afraid to face Miller.

"Get behind me." Miller reached an arm out that moved me behind him.

"He's not going to—"

Miller's blue magic shot out but Caleb easily blocked it.

I'd seen this before. Miller was just testing him. Then Caleb's black magic came screaming for Miller who also deflected.

Being new, I couldn't even guess what spells they were throwing at each other but I wasn't going to sit here and let them waste our time.

"Stop it," I snapped then slid around Miller, putting myself between the two.

"Hazel, get behind me," he ground out.

"No." I shook my head. "Caleb's not going to hurt me." I turned to Caleb and added, "Are you?"

Caleb's nostrils flared before he answered. "No."

"Exactly. Then you're not going to have a fucking stare down with Miller either."

Caleb's shoulders relaxed. "Miller?"

"Yes, Miller." I took a deep breath, glanced at my boyfriend then hurried over to Caleb. "He's taking us to Echo Valley. Come with us."

"I can't."

"You can. You're just afraid to."

Caleb scowled at me like I was being a pest. Maybe I was. I didn't care but he didn't belong here anymore than I did. "I'm not afraid," he said as he focused on me. "But I wouldn't be welcome anywhere near a light coven."

"They don't own the valley."

He let out a quick breath. "No, they don't but the shadow coven will be coming after me. I can't fight an entire coven on my own."

Now it was my turn to furrow my brows as I waved Miller over. Nellie and Gia came with him. "Is there a way to undo the dark magic?"

"What?" he asked like he couldn't have known what I meant. "Is there a way for a dark witch to become a light witch?"

Before Miller could answer, Gia glanced at him then said, "Yes, there is. It's not easy and it might be a little painful. I've heard the dark witch has to prove themselves, make sacrifices, etc. And there's no guarantee a light coven would accept a former dark witch but it could happen."

Locking me gaze with Caleb, I said, "See? Come with us. You helped the four of us at risk to yourself. Let us help you."

Before he answered, Caleb met Miller's gaze and it was like the two of them were having a silent conversation. Then I knew they had been when Miller said, "If Hazel trusts you, I'll trust you. For now."

Yeah. That tracked. Miller wasn't going to assume this dark witch was a decent person without proof and that was understandable. But right now, he needed to trust me.

"Let's go." Caleb turned on his heel and led the way.

Everyone had been at the ceremony so the camp itself was dead. It wasn't hard for us to slip out without anyone noticing.

"Where are we headed?" Caleb asked.

Miller tightened his grip on my hand and began to move almost faster than my shorter legs could go.

"We have some cars hidden a few miles away." He cleared his throat. "I've got her. We're headed to the car. There are three extras with me."

It took me a while to understand that he wasn't talking to me but someone else. "Who were you talking to?"

"Oliver came up with a communication spell. So that we can hear each other when we're in a fight." He explain and I had no idea that was something even possible.

"No tech?" Caleb asked.

Miller shook his head but kept his pace running smoothly.

"That's a really good idea."

Miller's muscles tensed but he didn't say anything back.

Obviously, those two were going to need some get to know you time. Though I could see how it looked to Miller. He came to get me and I don't want to leave without another man. Someone he doesn't know.

Once I had the chance to explain things, he'd understand. Or maybe he wouldn't. But as much as I was Miller's, he'd have to get used to the fact that Caleb was my friend.

"Fuck," Caleb spat the shot a dark magic ball at

someone I hadn't even noticed. The man went down with a thud that I hoped to never heard again. "Guess that means I for sure can't go back to the shadow coven."

When he saw the curiosity on my face he added, "That was the assistant director."

"Of the camp?" Miller asked.

Caleb chuckled. "Of the coven. They're about to get a whole lot angrier."

The five of us slowed down a little once we had the cover of trees. I thought we'd walked maybe a mile before we saw another person. My hand tightened on Miller's when I saw the shadows and heard the voices.

At least until I heard Oliver say, "Admit it. You're jealous of my skills."

Followed by Luken's, "Fuck off."

Then the five of us were there with Oliver, Luken, and Miller's dad.

"Wait," I said after they told me how glad they were to have me back. "If was just the four of you."

Oliver chuckled. "You're surprised, Hazel? You knew we were badasses."

"But that's... a while coven."

"No it's not," Caleb but in for the first time, though he was keeping his physical distance and the way he held himself said he was ready to defend if necessary. "It's not the whole coven. Honestly, I don't even know how many members there are."

Mr. Campbell pushed through us all until he was standing in front of Caleb. "And who do we have here? A dark witch, Miller?" But his eyes never wavered.

"Hazel didn't want to leave without him," Miller explained.

"Oh so Miller's got some competition..." That was Oliver always trying to be funny but starting trouble instead.

"There's no competition," I assured everyone. "But Caleb kept us safe in there and I don't think he wants to be a dark witch. So everyone can calm down. He helped us. We're taking him with us." I shook out of Miller's hand so that I could stand between Mr. Campbell and Caleb. "Now, the three of us have a tracker in our arm and if we don't get it out soon, they're going to follow us anyway."

Mr. Campbell stared him down another minute, narrowed his eyes, then said, "Fine. I don't want any trouble out of you." It was such a dad thing to say.

"And you won't get any."

Miller's dad pushed away then over his shoulder said, "We can't go back to Echo Valley. Not until we have those trackers out at least. We need the equipment. I know where we're going so follow me.

Which we did. Until we were standing beside two cars. Miller's and another that I didn't recognize. Oliver and Luken climbed in with Miller's dad while the rest of us got cozy in Miller's car. I was in the font with him where he could continue to hold my hand while Nellie and Gia squeezed into the back with Caleb.

"I'm going to do a spell," Caleb said once we were on the road. "You're going to see it so I thought I should warn you."

"A spell for what?" Miller asked.

"To cloak us from dark magic. It won't last long though."

"We can use the head start.

A black fog like smoke enveloped our car and Mr. Campbells and Caleb was right to warn us. Miller murmured something that I knew wasn't for us and I wished I could hear the response he got.

If we weren't going home, we were at least one step closer and none of that mattered because now that I was with Miller, I knew he wasn't going to let them take me again.

At least for now, I was safe.

I couldn't say that about the future.

14

MILLER

It took a while before we stopped in front of this run down looking cabin that I'd noticed was in the opposite direction of Echo Valley. The camp was probably almost halfway between here and there and I had to assume that Dad wanted us as far away from Echo Valley for several reasons.

One, it would put distance between the shadow coven and his wife.

Two, Echo Valley was probably the first place they'd go to look for us.

"This should buy us some time," Dad said as he got the door opened. "I'm going to start the generator."

"You have gas for that?" I asked him while

holding Hazel's hand tightly in mine. Almost too tight but with her, there was no such thing.

I had her back and I wasn't letting her the fuck go for anything.

"It's solar powered so as long as there's been sunlight, it should've been filling."

After he left, I turned to Luken and Oliver. "He possibly saved our lives." It was the only way I could explain Caleb. "Hazel wouldn't leave without him. These two..." Now I pointed to Gia and Nellie who were holding each other tightly. "Were her room-mates. They didn't drink the dark magic or whatever and didn't pledge the shadow coven. I'm told."

"They didn't," Caleb spoke for the first time since we'd gotten here.

"Why should we trust him?" Oliver asked as if Caleb hadn't said a word.

"Because he helped us." Hazel stepped forward to stand up for the guy which didn't completely sit right with me. "He made sure we were all right."

"Yet you were still at the ceremony."

Caleb's jaw tightened. "That couldn't be helped. You want me to take on an entire coven by my fucking self?" He shook his head. "That's suicide."

"I would've done it," I told him. "For Hazel, without question."

He glanced at her which had me wanting to rip his eyeballs out of his head then looked back at me. "I'd say our relationships with Hazel are a bit different, yeah?"

I nodded. They better fucking have been. "Yeah." But I needed to get her alone for a minute. Make sure she was really all right and get my hands on her so that I believed she was all right.

After finding out the shit the shadow coven did to my mother and many other girls... if they fucking touched Hazel, I'd burn their shit to the ground. Fuck. I might do that anyway. "Speaking of, I need to see you for a minute."

Hazel didn't have to answer because I was pulling her toward one of the doors in the cabin. There were only two so I assumed one was a bedroom and another a bathroom. I pushed through one then pulled her inside behind him.

This was the bedroom.

Once I shut the door behind us, I pushed me against the wall gently.

"I have to make sure you're OK." That wasn't my normal voice. This one was dark and desperate.

"You can check anything you want."

I pushed my fingers roughly into her hair, cupping her cheeks before my mouth crashed down onto mine. While I captured the groan that vibrated her chest, all she could do was brace her hands against my chest.

"We're going to put up some wards," Luken called out probably because he heard me push her against the wall and because he was my friend. He knew me.

He knew what I'd need to reassure myself that she was here. And what I'd want the moment I saw her. The outside door shut loudly before I broke the kiss.

"Are you OK?" I asked her feeling like I'd just run a marathon.

"Yes." At least she sounded as breathless as I did.

"Are you sure? Did they..." The question burned like fucking fire in my stomach. "Hurt you? Touch you?"

She gave my hair a pull so that we were eye to eye. "No, Miller. I don't think that's why they wanted me. I don't really know why but Caleb does."

My mood darkened. I wasn't so sure we should trust Caleb in the first place. He was there because my girl had a big heart not because I wanted him there. The Fae told me. That wasn't something I wanted Hazel to worry about.

"Has he told you?"

She shook her head quickly. "He can't. It's some kind of dark magic binding. If you already know, he can talk about it but I don't know and haven't guessed yet."

Fuck. I really didn't want to be the one to tell her but if she had to know, it had to be me.

It just wouldn't be now.

"Why..." She wet her lips quickly. "Why did you ask if they'd touched me."

I dropped my forehead to hers. "Because they've done it before. My mom was one of them."

Her breath caught in her chest as she brought her hands to my cheeks. "What?"

Take a small moment before moving away from her just enough, I told her, "While you were gone I found out that someone from the shadow coven drugged and raped my mom. That's how she got me."

Her brows furrowed. "That would mean your Dad..."

"Isn't my biological father but he's still my dad."

"I'm so sorry," she said quietly then took a deep breath. "They didn't do anything to me. You can give a thorough inspection. What do you need?"

That was an easy answer. "You."

She cocked her head to the side and gave me a

tiny grin. "You have me, Miller. You can have me right now if that's what you need."

That go ahead was all I'd been waiting for. I was back kissing her, running my hands over her curves through this ridiculous black dress. I undid the zipper so that I could at least pull it down her shoulders and expose her breasts to the air and me. Then I slid both of my hands up the outside of each of her thighs until I was high enough to bring her panties down.

My fingers crawled back up until I found that warm paradise between her legs. As my tongue pushed into her mouth, my fingers teased her opening before I slid one in. She dropped her head back against the wall with a thud.

Everyone out there better still have been outside. This was just for her and me.

I circled her clit again and again until I brought her to the edge. Then I stopped, got my own jeans unbuttoned and my erection free so that I could push into her.

We both groaned. It'd only been days but that wasn't what this was about. This was a way to get rid of all that fear we'd both had while she was gone and show our love. As I pushed into her again and again, I slid my hand between us to press her clit. It only took twice before she was coming undone and I was right behind her.

That might not have been my finest work but it'd gotten the job done. We were both breathless when I finally pulled out her. It has also been the first time I'd been inside her without a condom and it was going to be hell to have something between us again.

When she realized that too, she looked up at me with wide eyes. "I'm going to have to stop at the bathroom."

"Yeah." I kissed her gently before standing up again. "Sorry about the mess."

She chuckled and shook her head. "Somehow I don't think you are."

Hazel was right. I wasn't sorry. Couldn't be sorry for what we'd just done. But I would take care of her. "As soon as we get back, there's a potion I can make you so that you don't..."

"Get pregnant?" she asked which made me nod. Hazel had pulled her dress up and spun around, moving her hair out of the way so that I could zip it for her. Made me really hope it was one of the other girls that had done this for her when she first put the thing on. I nodded. "Like a magical morning after pill?"

"Basically."

"I'm on birth control but it never hurts to be doubly sure." Hazel turned back to me. "Have you had to use that before."

I groaned. This wasn't something I wanted to discuss with her but there wasn't a way around it. "Yes. Once. In high school. Condom broke."

"And here I thought I was special."

She said it with sarcasm. I heard it, I knew it but when she turned toward the door, I pulled her back to me. "You are, Hazel. You're the most precious thing to me."

Her face softened and she cocked her head to the side. "I know Miller. I was teasing."

One more kiss and a stop for her at the restroom and we were on our way to find the others. They were outside, each walking from a separate direction toward the front door. Except Gia and Nellie. They were huddled together like wounded dogs following my father at a distance.

"That didn't take long," Oliver said as soon as he saw us which earned him a slap to the back of the head from my dad.

Yeah. They all knew why I'd needed to take Hazel into that room. Well, maybe not everyone. I didn't know what Nellie, Gia, Gia, or Caleb knew.

After narrowing her eyes on Oliver, Hazel said,

"Thank you Oliver, Luken, and Mr. Campbell for coming to get me. Get us."

"First, call me Cooper," Dad told her reminding me that those two had never met. I just hadn't gotten around to it. "Second, my son loves you which means I'll do anything to keep you safe."

My girl blushed and tucked a piece of hair behind her ear. The wind wasn't awful but there was a breeze.

"What's that?" I pointed to the box that my father was holding.

"We have to get their trackers out." Then he walked toward the cabin.

Right. The trackers the shadow coven had put on them so that we couldn't magically hide them. Fucking perfect.

Dad got his things set up on the table. There was several bottles of saline, antibiotic ointment, what looked like a scalpel, bandages. Then he looked at the girls.

Nellie and Gia were shaking like scared little puppies and it had to be because they didn't know us. We'd earn their trust.

"I'll go first," Hazel volunteered as she stepped forward. Then she looked at her friends. "I'll go first so you'll both know it's not that bad."

Hazel took a seat at the table while Dad sanitized the knife. Why he had those things in the car, I didn't know and thought it possible that I didn't want to.

"I'll do it," I told him before he sat in front of her.

I took the seat he'd been about to and turned Hazel's arm over. Once I found the small mark on her arm where it'd been injected, I cleaned it off and reached for the knife. Dad handed me the knife carefully.

I made the cut as quickly as I could because the small cry that came from my girl was about more than I could stand. Then I held my hand over the opening and called on my power. Despite Hazel's cries, the tracker was in my hand in seconds. I handed the fucker off the Luken then cleaned her up and put a waterproof bandage on it.

Done. Dad could do the other two.

While he worked on the girls, I took Hazel under my arm.

"It's not going to take long before they get here," Caleb told me.

"Why haven't they yet? With the tracker..."

"It's the cloaking spell I did. It's worn off now so we need to get these taken care of then watch for them."

"How long are we staying here, Dad?" I asked.

"Just overnight. Then we can head back to the valley." He put the snug bandage on Gia's arm then Nellie stepped forward. "Figure they'll be here before morning, then we can head out."

"Wait." Hazel had been leaning her weight against my but now snapped up straight. "You think they're going to find us?"

Caleb furrowed his brows. "I know they are. But it's better to fight a small group out here then lead the whole damn thing to your doorstep."

"He's right," I told her before she could protest. "Better here than where my mom and Danna are." They were the only two people I truly gave a shit about still in Echo Valley. My circle was small but we were mighty."

"So how are we going to fight them?" She started to pace. "Gia, Nellie, and I are still bound. How do we undo that?"

The question was directed at Caleb and I tried to warn him nonverbally but he either didn't pick up or didn't care. That information wasn't something she needed to know.

"Either your parents counteract their spell," he told her. "Or..."

"Or what?" When he didn't answer quick enough she repeated it. "Or what, Caleb?"

"Or if they die."

Her eyes widened at the thought of her parents death being the only way to unbind her without their permission.

"Trust me," I told her. "I know how you feel about that. It's the only reason they're still alive. But we will figure it out. Right now, we need a plan for the shadow coven for when they get here."

That was where our focus needed to be. Everything else could wait.

"Hey." I tugged or over then moved away from the group a few feet. They'd absolutely be able to hear us but it gave the appearance of a little privacy. "What's going on?"

"Just... I don't have a home anymore," she said quietly.

"The fuck you don't," I told her gently. "You have a home wherever I am. Period. You don't have to worry about this."

She sniffed back those tears. "I don't have my home, Miller. Now I find out that I can't even have my full powers unless they're dead? That's insane."

"I know. I know it is. But we will get that figured out."

Now that the trackers were out, Luken took them in his hand, wrapped the other over the top ten mumbled the words we'd used to make questions on the math test disappear. With a quick flash of light, he opened his hands to nothing inside. He'd gotten rid of those awful thinks.

We'd decided to have the girls take the bedroom then the rest of us would sleep in shifts so that we could potentially alert the others if those following us decided to show their faces.

All I wanted was some shadow coven blood on my hands and I truly felt like today was going to be that day.

15

HAZEL

I LAID in the bed in the cabin with Gia on one side of
me and Nellie on the other, staring at the ceiling.
Everyone had to be out of their minds to think I was
just going to go to sleep.

We'd left the camp in a hurry which meant the
three of us girls were still wearing the damn ceremony dresses that, if not for the purpose they served,
would've been really pretty, actually. Still didn't
mean I wanted to sleep in the damn thing.

Every sound in the night sent my heart on a race
that it couldn't win. It didn't matter that those noises
were likely one of the guys walking around the cabin
as they looked for signs of danger. All I could think
about was what if it wasn't.

What if a team from the shadow coven followed us with the intent of bringing us back?

Going there was no good and I felt confident in the fact that Miller would die before he'd let that happen and so would his father by extension. It wasn't that I thought Cooper would die for me but he definitely would Miller so I'd be leaving a body count in my wake.

But losing Miller wasn't something I thought I could handle.

By the time the sun had come up, I'd barely fallen asleep.

When I heard someone yelling out in the main room for everyone else to wake up, I thought I was dreaming. Then the door to the cabin slammed against something causing a loud bang and I knew it wasn't.

"Hazel, wake up." Nellie shook me hard which made me jump up.

"What's going on?" I hurried to the window.

"I don't know, but I didn't want to go out there without you."

I nodded then hurried from the room, not caring at all what I looked like.

No one was in the main room so we hurried to the open door and stepped outside.

All of the guys were busy fighting a group of people I'd never seen before. A loud clap of thunder made me duck on instinct.

Miller threw a vial of purple liquid which caused a haze that made it very hard to see. "Stay back," he yelled and I didn't need two guesses as to who he was talking about.

The three of us had powers, sure. They were bound and what we did have were so new that we probably wouldn't have been much help. We stood there, tightly holding on to each other probably thinking the same thing.

We weren't going back no matter what.

"It looks like..." Gia trailed off and glanced around. "Like they're throwing different colored energy at each other."

"It does."

This was something I had no experience with but when I saw Caleb get his hands on one of the shadow coven guys, he didn't use magic to snap his neck.

My heart raced as my stomach turned. I'd never seen someone killed before. Yet there was a certainty that Caleb didn't need to touch the person to kill them. He'd done it when we were leaving the camp.

Did that mean this was personal to him? That

he'd wanted to do it with his bare hands. I'd remember to ask later.

Oliver flew through the air but landed on his feet or well... in more of a superhero pose then he lifted his hands and pushed a man against a tree without even touching him. The man screamed and tried to lift his own hands to retaliate but couldn't.

The force of the wind either suffocated him or crushed his chest because when Oliver pulled his hands back, the man fell to the ground and didn't get back up.

That was when I squeezed my eyes closed so that I couldn't have to see anymore. Gia was crying while Nellie was stone. None of us wanted to witness any of this.

As quickly as it'd started, everything went silent which made me peek. The guys were all walking toward Miller. Some words I couldn't hear were said then he turned and came toward us.

"Are you OK?" he asked all three of us but was only looking at me.

"Physically, yes," I told him.

"Psychologically..." Gia shuttered. "Maybe never."

Miller nodded and wet his bottom lip. "We got them all which means they can't report back. But it won't be too long before others come looking for them. Caleb says we should get out of here because they'll send more."

"Where will we go?" I asked, my eyes burning with tears that I wasn't going to allow to fall.

"Home." I raised an eyebrow. "My home. Our home. Whatever. Now that your trackers are out, we can shield you. Caleb says he can also do something to help. But we're headed there. You three need to eat and change." He looked me from top to bottom, appreciating the way the dress hugged my curves. "And decompress a little. You'll be safe there."

I swallowed hard then nodded.

They had the three of us go inside while they cleaned up their mess and I didn't want to think about what that might've meant. So we waited until they were ready for us then climbed back into the cars like we had to get here.

I rode in the front with Miller with my head leaning against the window. Everything was quickly catching up to me and if I didn't sleep tonight, I wasn't going to be any good to anyone. My eyelids were heavy, the comfort of Miller holding my hand and the knowledge that these moments were probably some of the last calm ones we'd have for a while, all helped lull me off to sleep.

"Hazel," Miller's gently voice attempted to rouse me from the comfortable sleep I'd fallen into. "Hazel. We're home."

My eyes sprung open to find that we were in the driveway of Miller's parent's house and an honest smile crossed my face.

This was familiar and the more space between us and the camp, the better I felt.

"Come on," he said gently. "My mom has lunch for everyone."

The idea of food made my stomach growl loudly which caused him to chuckle. It wasn't like they starved us at the camp but we'd been gone twelve hours now. It was time to eat.

I slid out of his car and he wrapped an arm around my waist as we made our way to the back door where Nellie, Gia, and Caleb were waiting.

All of this was unfamiliar to those three. I was the only person they really knew and we'd only known each other days. I guess the saying about bonds being formed during times of crisis were true.

"It's OK," I told them once I got there. "This place will be safe." Caleb raised an eyebrow. "Or safer anyway."

"It'll be safe," Miller promised. "We have a few tricks up our sleeves."

As we crossed over the threshold, this feeling washed over me like thousands of tiny fingers giving me a slight static shock. That had never happened before. But when Caleb tried to follow, he grunted as it looked like he was more going through a lightning storm.

I spun around and tried to go to him but Miller grabbed me around my waist to stop me. "Hang on," he said close to my ear.

Caleb took a step back, his chest heaving as he tried to catch his breath. "What the hell was that?"

"It's a ward," Miller's mother, who I hadn't met yet came forward. I'd seen her around town and at school sometimes but had never spoken to her. "It's meant to keep dark magic from crossing the threshold. She looked up at Miller. "It worked."

"Wait." I held my hand up. "That means he can't come in here?" I turned to Miller with my eyebrows raised. That wasn't going to work for me.

"He can." Miller took a vial of red liquid from his mother's outstretched hand. "He just has to take a sip of this first."

Miller walked it over to Caleb who was so careful not to cross that threshold with his hand and took the vial from Miller. After sipping from it, he took a deep breath and crossed through. This time, his spine straightened a little but he was able to make it into the house.

"What the hell was that?" Caleb asked and I wanted to know the answer to that as well.

"Dark magic ward," his mom told him. "Keeps dark magic out better than anything I've ever seen."

Caleb furrowed his brows. "Why didn't we use this at the cabin?"

"You need Fae blood," Miller explained. "We don't have a lot of it and we don't have any Fae laying around waiting to be blooded. But we're using it for this house so make sure you sip that first." He took a step forward, crowding into Caleb who didn't look like he cared at all. "And you'd better not share it with anyone else."

Wrapping my hand around Miller's arm, I pulled him back. "He's not going to. Now, I'm hungry. Can we eat?"

Miller gazed down at me with a hard jaw that softened as soon as our gazes met. "Yeah, baby. We can do that."

The group of us found seats around his parent's table where his mom had so many sandwiches already set out. Along with small bags of chips and fresh veggies. Miller, Luken, and Oliver got everyone something to drink before actually sitting down themselves. Then Miller introduced the four of us to his mom.

She greeted everyone then homed in on me. "Hazel, it's very nice to meet you." Her tone made me realize that Miller had told his parents about me and not just in the way that the person he was supposed to be training had been taken.

He must have told them about us and now I wished we were alone so I could ask them.

"So we probably have a little bit of a breather," Cooper said before taking a huge bite of his sandwich.

"Not much of one," Caleb countered. "They're not going to like the mess we left at the cabin."

"I agree." Cooper took a drink before speaking again. "So we need to spend our time wisely. I have a backup plan for when the shit hits the fan again but what do we need to do first?"

"Looks like the girls could use a shower and some clothes," Eden offered up.

"And some sleep," Miller added. When I tried to protest he came in close and whispered, "I know you were awake more of last night."

Well, that I couldn't argue with. But how did he know?

"For clothes," I said instead. "We could go to my

house and get mine. The three of us are fairly close in size."

Miller had started to shake his head before I'd gotten the whole sentence out. "You're not leaving this house."

I raised my eyebrows in surprise. He'd sounded a lot like a dad telling me I was grounded.

"You sound like you just grounded her," Caleb told him with a smirk. It was like he'd pulled the idea out of my head.

"I wouldn't comment on what I say to Hazel if I were you."

This felt like something that was going to be turned into something bigger. No thank you. "Let's just stop right there." I slid my hand into Miller's so that he'd be able to feel me beside him. Logically, he knew I was there but now, he could feel me. "But he's right. You can't keep me prisoner in this house. Is this where I'm staying right now anyway?"

Miller's brows slammed down. "Of course. Where the fuck else would you go?"

I pointed toward the back door. "Your apartment?"

"Hazel," Eden's sweet voice spoke before Miller could respond. "We think it's a better idea for you three to stay here. We have the Fae ward going. It's the safest it can be."

"What about everyone else? Will we all fit?" I asked then quickly added, "I'm not taking someone's bed."

"So my thought was that Nellie and Gia could share the guest room. You and Miller could stay in his old room and Caleb could take Miller's apartment."

"It's the best layout we could come up with," Cooper added. "Given… everything. We thought Caleb would be most comfortable in a space of his own."

"One that's not protected from the shadow coven." Caleb folded his arms across his chest and nodded.

"We didn't think you'd need it," Cooper answered honestly. "If they show up you can tell them you're playing double agent, which you are, just not for them so even if they try to truth it out of you, it is the truth."

Caleb took a moment then nodded. "Makes as much sense as anything else."

Luken cleared his throat. "Oliver and I will sleep in the living room if that's OK with you all. We're not comfortable going to our own places until we know everyone is safe."

Miller gave them the guy nod of appreciation. It made me wonder if my best friend would've done that for me. But it wasn't like I could've called her to ask. Who knew what she thought happened to me.

He leaned into me and whispered in my ear. "We have to stay here." I nodded because yeah, given the circumstances, we did.

"But I can't wear this dress forever." I motioned down to the offending item. "We could just go, pack some things up and come back." This was a plea to my boyfriend. If he could get behind this idea then it could happen.

"Or, or…" He held up a finger. "And hear me out… I could go and pack some things up."

I sighed. "Miller, I want to go get my things. You'll probably bring the wrong things."

"How would I do that?"

I cocked my head to the side and narrowed my eyes. "Probably bring anything with lace on it but leave behind something like jeans." Then I remembered where I was and slapped a hand over my mouth as his mother snorted.

How embarrassing. I couldn't believe I'd just said that.

"You might be right," he gave me then looked to

his dad where they clearly had a silent conversation. Finally, after what seemed like forever, he nodded. "Fine. We'll go."

I furrowed my brows. "Like all of us?"

"No." He chuckled. "The fewer to draw attention the better. You, me, Luken, and Oliver."

"And me," Caleb added. Before Miller could disagree he said, "Listen, I'm going to have a lot of shit to make up for given my entire life up to this point and I started the day that I kept those three... well, four... out of shit at the camp. I'm not stopping now."

Four.

It was the first time we'd really acknowledge that Juniper was part of the shadow coven and therefore on the other side of this whole thing. Though I wouldn't look at her like an enemy. She'd been our friend and she'd made a choice.

Miller mulled it over then agreed. Caleb would go with us. Nellie and Gia would stay with Miller's parents.

"Are you two OK with this?" I asked because they didn't know these people at all. Neither did I really but if Miller said they'd be safe, I trusted him.

"Absolutely," Nellie answered for the both of them. "In fact, if we could just stay here cloaked with light magic and protected by Fae blood forever, I say, let's do that."

I snorted because I'd thought the same thing briefly but that was no life. Eventually, we needed to be able to do things.

We just had to do this first without the shadow coven finding us.

16

MILLER

LUKEN, Oliver, and I shoved potions in our pockets like they were loading up for war. Since Hazel wasn't a fully trained witch yet, She wouldn't understand why we could do magic with the wave of our hands or flicks of our wrists yet still used potions for some things.

I wanted to explain it all but now wasn't the time. She'd just have to trust us.

Caleb and Hazel stood back waiting for us to be ready. This time, Dad wasn't coming with us. It had been decided that he would be of better use here with his wife and the girls if anything should happen. Though he was confident the ward Mom had made with the Fae blood would hold.

Then the five of us headed out.

As we climbed into my car, Luken, Oliver, and Caleb in the back, Hazel and me in the front, she asked the question that I'd seen working its way around her brain when we were getting ready. "Shouldn't one of you stay with your parents?"

Immediately, I shook my head as I hit the gas to get us going. "Nah. My parents have this. Plus the house is as protected as it could be."

"Where'd you get the Fae blood?" Caleb asked causing Me to tense. Telling a dark magic practicing member of the shadow coven where we got Fae blood didn't sit right with me. However, Hazel trusted the guy and I'd determined to do the same. The trust would only go so far but for now, this was what we were doing.

I glanced in the rearview mirror then at Hazel who gave me an encouraging nod.

"Dad and I tracked down a Fae that's been hiding from Hazel's parents for like twenty years."

"Hiding?" She asked sounding more confused with every single thing I told her. "From my parents?"

"Yeah. It's a whole thing." I shifted uncomfortably then took a corner a little too fast. Telling Hazel about the deal her parents made wasn't something I was looking forward to. It was something that needed to be done but not here with three guys listening in. "I'll explain it all but I don't think right now is the time."

Well, she didn't love that. She scowled and wrapped her hands over her stomach which meant I wasn't holding on to her anymore. Since we'd gotten her back, I wanted to be touching her just so I could remind myself that she was there. She just wanted to know what I'd found out and I couldn't blame her however, I wasn't doing it here.

Hazel turned slightly in her seat to peer into the backseat. "Can everyone see that?"

At first, I wasn't sure what she meant but then I realized it was the thin black haze around our car that mean Caleb was doing something and if I had to guess it was a spell that meant the shadow coven couldn't see us.

"No." His gaze settled on her. "Only witches."

At least the good people of Echo Valley wouldn't think some kind of vapor had taken over the town which meant they wouldn't activate the emergency response alarm. There was something about the way Caleb looked at her that always had me on edge.

Now, I trusted my girl. Hazel wasn't the kind of person to cheat but they'd clearly formed a bond in that camp and it was one I just knew was going to be a problem for me. She could be friends with who she wanted. I wasn't her keeper but I didn't like her having any kind of bond with any man that wasn't me.

It was a possessive thing and before she'd been taken, I probably wouldn't have batted an eye. Her being gone made me want to hover over her and bark at any other guy who got too close. Especially knowing what her parents had planned for her.

I came to a stop two blocks from her house and said, "Luken?"

"On it." my best friend hopped from the car and jogged over to Hazel's house or at least to where we couldn't see him anymore.

When she furrowed my brows, I decided to let the rest of us, or at least her, in on what was happening. Oliver would've known and I didn't really care what Caleb knew. "He's checking the house. Make sure your parents aren't there."

Her mouth formed a soft o as if she'd forgotten that her parents were still something we had to deal with. None of us had any idea where they were at this point but they'd know she wasn't at the camp anymore. Everyone knew by now. Soon, Luken jogged back to my window. "It's clear. Doesn't look like anyone's been there since we were."

"You were at my house?" she asked.

Luken leaned down and peered through the window. "Yeah. We were trying to find you."

"All right." I let out a deep sigh. "We'll go in but Hazel, I need you to listen to us. If your parents show up, I'm getting you out of there no matter what. Got it?" No one was going to touch her as long as I had breath in my body. She nodded. "They're not getting their hands on you again."

There was an intensity inside of me that I knew meant she'd understand that I'd kill anyone I had to if it meant keeping her safe but it was an intensity that she wouldn't understand. She might've thought it was because I loved her or didn't want her taken against her will again.

But really it was because I didn't want some damn Fae thinking he could have her. That he'd just show up and take her.

Fuck that.

The five of us got out of my car and headed to Hazel's where Luken already had the front door unlocked for us. As we approached the house, I stepped aside with Hazel so that the other three could enter. Then once we were in, I turned around, waved my hand and sealed the door.

"I don't understand how you all do that with just

the flick of your hand," Hazel whispered as she pushed forward.

"You'll get there." It was all in the training and she seemed to forget that Oliver and I had been doing magic since we were kids. Luken learned as a teenager but he still had like six years of experience. Hazel had only known she was a witch for weeks.

We stuck together no matter how much I didn't want Luken, Oliver, or Caleb in her bedroom. Especially Caleb. There was a suspicion niggling at the back of my mind that I might've been able to trust Caleb with Hazel's safety but his reasoning was a little too close to mine.

"What do you need?" Oliver asked once we were all in her room.

Being my first time in Hazel's room, I turned to take it in. It was crisp, white, modern. Nothing too overdone. She had a huge bed in the middle that I could've thought of a hundred ways to use, bookshelves that took up an entire wall like her own little library, a desk on the other wall that filled with a mess of things. Where the rest of her room was immaculate, the desk was a mess.

"There are a couple of large bags in the closet," she told him. "I want to take as much of my clothes as I can so that Nellie and Gia have things to wear until we can get their own things."

Oliver headed into the closet then came out quickly with the bags she'd mentioned.

"I basically just want to take anything I can fit." She pointed at the dresser. "I'll do the dresser if you guys want to grab things from the closet." She turned away then came back. "You can leave anything that looks too dressy but I need to take some shoes."

"Got it." Oliver and Luken went into the closet while Hazel moved over to the dresser. Caleb slid over to the windows and peered out like he was watching for anything out of the ordinary.

"You don't want help with the dresser?" I asked when she pulled open the first drawer.

"Well, you can help." She kept her voice down so that no one else would hear her when at least Caleb would've been able to. "But this is where personal items are." Her jade eyes looked up at me. "Panties... bras..."

A smile spread over my lips. "Got it." She didn't want anyone else to see the things that I got to. Couldn't have agreed with her more.

She took two hand fulls then headed over to the bags. I grabbed everything else from that drawer, knowing that I'd make sure my old dresser was cleaned out for her.

"Your parents are really all right with me staying in your room with you?" she asked almost shyly that I couldn't help but grin.

She was too fucking sweet.

"Hazel." I ran my hand up her back then down again. "I'm a grown man. My parents know we have sex. Of course they wouldn't care if you stayed with me."

Her eyes widened. "They know? What do you mean they know? You told them?"

"They know him," Luken offered before dumping a bunch of clothes into the other bag.

Her face pinked up as she realized everyone could hear her even though she tried her hardest for the conversation to stay between the two of us. I snorted though I didn't mean to.

"I don't even want to know what that means," she said through clenched teeth.

"Remember him in high school?" Luken asked causing Hazel to scowl again. "It's not like he changed."

She turned to me and raised an eyebrow. "He doesn't know what he's talking about," I assured her.

I had changed. I only wanted Hazel. No one else mattered.

It was like we'd forgotten Caleb was there until he said, "I thought you were a virgin."

Anger raged within me. Why the fuck did he think she was a virgin? Why the fuck had they even talked about that? And why the fuck had Hazel lied?

"Want me to get her V-card out of my wallet?" I asked him when I really shouldn't have. What happened between Hazel and me was private. Just for us.

She snorted this time. "You don't actually have that."

"Baby, I know. But it was funnier this way." I ran my hand in circles on her back.

She took a deep breath as she turned to Caleb. "I lied. One of the girls said that the last one who said she wasn't a virgin disappeared. No one knew what happened to her so it was safer to pledge my purity."

He wet his lips and shook his head. "Do you know what would've happened to you if they found out you lied?"

She dropped her hands to the side. "No. Because no one tells you shit in there."

Caleb was about to respond when we heard a

noise downstairs. No one way anyone got through the seal but fuck. We had to be sure.

"I'll go," Caleb offered then slipped out the door quietly.

The rest of us hurried to finish getting her things and were ready when he came back to say that there was nothing down there. But it was the reminder we all needed. We had to leave. Shouldn't have been here this long as it were.

That had been stupid on my part and risked exposing Hazel to the dark Fae or the shadow coven.

17

MILLER

WE GOT out of Hazel's house without an issue. Whatever we'd heard was nothing. Caleb said he'd checked the entire first floor and it looked exactly as it had when we got there.

Arriving back home, we found Nellie and Gia in robes, having already taken a shower. They helped Hazel get her things settled in my room while I went to my apartment to grab things of my own. Though I left some so that Caleb could change if he wanted to. It was also the best time for Luken and Oliver to head home, shower, and bring back bags of their own. No idea how long we were going to be holed up in my parent's house.

Once they were all worked out, Hazel took a

deep breath and said it was her turn to shower and I couldn't agree more.

When I entered the bathroom after she got her water running, the black dress was on the floor in a pile along with what she'd been wearing underneath. I flipped the lock on the door then asked, "Is it OK that I'm in here?"

She pulled the curtain back. Her hair was hanging in wet strands around her and she'd never looked more beautiful. "Of course it is."

"How in here can I be?"

"What do you mean?"

I cocked my head to the side then reached back and pulled my shirt over my head in one motion. Her eyes widened as she tried to fight a smile.

"I need to get clean, too," I told her.

She snorted. "Somehow I think if you come in here you'll be getting dirty. Not clean."

She wasn't wrong. I slid my jeans and boxers down as she shut the curtain again then climbed into the shower with her. Hazel was already wet and warm when I slid my hands over her shoulder. She moved aside so that I could step under the spray but then I brought her back to where she was.

With a washcloth in hand, I squeezed a little body wash on it then ran it over her shoulder. My cock was already so hard that I didn't think it could get harder and was tapping against the curve of her lower back. She knew it was there, too.

Once I rinsed her skin, I trailed kissed from her shoulder to her neck. She dropped her head to the side and sighed. "You know your parents are downstairs."

"Yup. Downstairs. Not in here."

I continued washing down her back then reached around and ran the cloth over her breasts and down her stomach, causing her breathing to increase. After wringing the cloth out, I set it on the edge of the tub and made the same trek with my hand. As my hand went further down her stomach, Hazel leaned back into me and sighed a satisfied sound.

This was me taking care of her. Showing her that I loved her even if she hadn't said it back. She loved me. I didn't have to question that but what I wouldn't give to hear those words out of her mouth. For now, I'd be content in knowing it.

Her skin was silk soft, wet and warm, when I pushed my hand between her legs. She moved them further apart and it was like she hadn't even intended to do it.

She was so fucking soft everywhere.

When my fingers circled her clit, her breath caught before she turned her head so that I could kiss her and kiss her I did. Her fingers pushed into my hair as I pulled her harder against my check. I wanted her to come undone and it was my mission to make it happen.

I swirled three more times, bringing out the quietest moan, that I thought she did on purpose because she was worried someone downstairs would hear us.

Then I pushed a finger inside her and let my thumb circle her clit. After a couple of strokes, I added a second. With my tongue in her mouth, fingers in her pussy, and thumb floating over her clit, it was only minutes before she tightened around my fingers and whimpered into my mouth. Once I'd gotten every drop of pleasure, I turned her, cupped her face and kissed her again.

"Wait," she said as she pulled back. I groaned because waiting was the hardest fucking thing for me to do right now. "Before you left your apartment." I knew exactly when she was referring to. "You told me you loved me."

I ran hand down her cheek. "I did." I swallowed hard. "I love you."

Her eyes filled with tears. "I didn't say it back."

"Know that too. You don't have to." Even if I wanted her to more than anything else in the world.

She swallowed hard and took a breath. "Then I was taken and I thought I'd never get the chance to. I love you, Miller. I loved you then and I love you now. I just don't want to chance you not hearing that from me."

I pulled her into my arms and tilted her head back. "I already knew but it feels so fucking good to hear you say it." Then I kissed her, my mouth working over hers in a methodical, demanding, almost bruising way.

She fucking loved me.

I pushed her back against the wall and nudged her so that she'd wrap her legs around my waist. She was too short for anything else.

"Wait." My cock was right at her entrance. One more second and I wouldn't have been able to wait. It would've been too late. "We already did this without a condom once. Is it smart to do it again?"

I leaned down and took one of her nipples between my lips before letting go with a pop. "I think it's the best idea."

She cocked her head to the side. "Miller."

"I can go get one," I told her. "But I have to make

you the potion when we get out of here anyway… we could go without this last time but it's up to you."

She ran her pink tongue over her bottom lip. "If you're sure that potion works."

"One hundred percent."

"Then I don't want anything between us."

I crashed my mouth into hers at the same time I pushed into her wetness. Fuck. That felt good. Like coming in out of the rain on a cold day to have a warm blanket wrapped around you and I almost lost it right there.

Instead, I pushed her back against the wall and moved away from her so that she was leaning a little. I held onto her hips as I pushed myself into her then back out. At this angle, I could see myself getting lost in her. But this wasn't going to last long. I was too turned on.

I pushed my thumb against her clit again, swirling with the help of the water until she came again. That was when I knew I could let myself go.

Once I stopped moving, she reached out and pulled herself up to me so that my hands were under her ass holding her up. And I was still inside her. She kissed me slow and steady, like she was trying to show me how she felt but she'd already done that.

Slowly, I pulled out of her and put her down onto her own feet.

Then I washed her again because she'd been right. Instead of getting clean, we'd gotten dirty.

We were both out of the shower, with wet hair and in new clean clothes when we headed back downstairs. The chattering of the others made it sound like we just had people over for a visit instead of the fact that we were hiding out from the shadow coven who wanted to give my girlfriend to a fucking dark fae so that she could be his source of dark power.

Before joining them, I slipped into the potion room with Hazel right behind me. She hopped up onto a nearby table, swinging her legs like she didn't have a care in the world as I grabbed everything I'd need to make this for her.

"You're good at this." I froze for a moment before continuing to work. "You know exactly what you need. Have you… needed it a lot?"

I didn't glance over my shoulder at her. "I wouldn't say a lot."

"What would you say?"

"I personally have needed it twice." I emptied the herbs that I'd just ground up into the bowl. "Once in high school when the condom broke and right now with you."

"Condom in high school, huh."

My stomach tightened but I kept working. Not looking at her was the easiest thing to do for this conversation. "I couldn't have you. I wanted to stop thinking about you so yeah... condom in high school."

"You know if you'd have talked to me, you could've had me then."

I groaned and pinched my eyes closed before forcing them open and adding the amount of water I needed. Then I shove the cork in and began to mix it. "I know that now. You hated my ass in high school so I didn't know it then."

She bit her lips together briefly as she tried to hold back a grin. "I hated you because you were a jerk. You were a jerk because you thought I hated you and couldn't have me. So it was kind of a fucked up carousel we were on."

"Yeah. It was."

With the potion complete, I pulled the cork off and handed the small bottle to her.

She looked at it with suspicion. "What's it going to taste like?" she asked and I would've as well. It was this weird green color that didn't look all that appetizing.

"I don't know." I wrapped my arms over my chest. "I've never taken a drink of it before. No idea what it'd do to me."

"If you only needed it twice, how are you so good at it?"

I snorted. "You remember Oliver and Luken in high school, too, right?"

She groaned and put the bottle to her lips, dropping her head back to drain the liquid. Her face scrunched up in disgust as she let out a gag. "That's nasty."

I chuckled but had heard that before. Telling her would've made it worse. "I supposed that's why people don't run around have unprotected sex and relying on this to take care of it. Imagine having to drink that every time you had sex."

"No thank you." She handed the bottle back to me. "Plus there's the whole STI situation. Condoms are good for that."

I froze with my hand halfway to the counter to set the bottle down. Fuck. We hadn't talked about that part.

"I'm not going to give you anything, Hazel."

"I didn't—"

Shaking my head, I cut her off. "No, I should've said something before. I'm not going to give you anything. I always wear a condom except when I'm with you apparently. But I've never had anything."

She reached out to pull me closer, ran her fingertips down my cheeks then settled her hands on the sides of my neck. "That wasn't what I was thinking at all. Besides, you love me. You wouldn't do anything to put me at risk. I know that. I trust you one hundred percent."

She definitely knew the right fucking thing to say. I couldn't help but kiss her. With my hands on her hips, I pulled her to the edge of the table so that her softness pressed against my growing hardness. If I could've, I would've taken her again right there.

But that would've made her uncomfortable and I wasn't going to do that. Instead, I brought that kiss to an end, finished cleaning up, washed the bottle out, then grabbed her hand so that we could join the others.

One night of normal was exactly what we needed though I didn't think it'd last long. My girl was tired and I was fucking itching to get her in bed even if it wasn't for sex. I always wanted Hazel. That was a fact but tonight, I wanted to hold her. I couldn't last night because she was sleeping with Nellie and Gia.

Tonight she was all mine. I was going to wrap myself around her to make sure that she knew that whatever was coming for us, I was going to stand between her and it.

Anything to keep her safe.

Before I could get her there though, I had to get Caleb settled in my apartment. He and I headed out there at almost midnight. Everyone's eyelids had started to droop. It'd been a long week.

"There are the basic protection wards up," I told him as we climbed the stairs.

"I'll take care of it." Caleb hadn't said much to me specifically. When he did speak it was mostly to Hazel. Otherwise, he'd kept pretty quiet unless directly asked a question.

I tried to put myself in his place. Leaving everything I'd known, my family, to help three girls that I didn't know. Turning my back on the only coven I'd ever been a part of. It couldn't be easy.

Even if his relationship with Hazel still bugged me. At least I now knew that the girls were supposed to be virgins which meant he wouldn't have tried anything like that with her.

"So you got to know Hazel at the camp?"

He nodded but didn't offer up much of anything else.

"Is there going to be a problem?" Best to just get the shit out there so we could deal with it.

"No." We pushed into my apartment so that he could have a look around.

"You don't talk much do you?"

He thought about that for a second then said, "I don't know you."

I snorted. "Yeah. How do you get to know people? You talk to them."

He sighed. "I'm dealing with a lot, OK? I just left my coven and I'm pretty sure you know what a big fucking deal that is. Not only will they be hunting my ass once they're less focused on her but it's the only life I've known."

Exactly what I'd been thinking. "If you're here to help us, you can become one of us. Either way, my family and I will help you. You made sure the woman that I love was safe. You didn't have to do that."

"I normally wouldn't do that," he confessed. "Honestly, I'm not really sure what it was about her but we haven't had anyone questioning anything for a long fucking time. When she did... it all started to make sense."

Nodding, I went over to check the cupboard to make sure there was some food in there. "That's Hazel for you."

"But you don't have to worry about me. Our friendship isn't like that. I just knew that I had to do what was best for her and the girls. I'm just pissed that Juniper slipped through my fingers. I thought for sure she was like the other three but nope. She made the pledge. Nothing I could do about it."

"The other roommate?" I asked. He nodded. "I heard she has a little brother. That's what made her do it."

He nodded again. "Yeah. She didn't want to leave him behind."

"What about you?" He shifted his weight like having the focus on him made him uncomfortable. "Did you leave family behind?"

His jaw tightened as he shook his head. "No. My mom died when I was little. Barely remember her. Since then, I've shifted from coven house to coven house until I was fifteen and moved into my own place."

My eyes narrowed. "You've been on your own since you were fifteen."

"Yeah."

"That's tough, man."

"We do what we have to."

I swallowed hard. Knowing how hard that must've been hit. "Well, there are some snacks in the cupboard, drinks in the fridge, and I left some clothes that should fit. We look about the same size. Use what you want. Should get you through the night. Mom will make a big breakfast in the morning, I'm sure. Just make sure to drink your Fae blood before you come in. The doors won't be locked so come over whenever you want."

He snorted. I figured it because I'd told him to drink the blood. Sounded awful by anyone's standards.

"Thanks again for protecting my girl." I moved to the door. When my hand was about to turn the knob he stopped me.

"Do you know why they want her to be a dark witch?" he asked which caused my entire body to freeze.

I looked over my shoulder at him but didn't take my hand off the knob. "Yeah."

"I'm bound from speaking of it to anyone that doesn't already know so if you know, you need to say it. It's the only thing that'll get past the binding."

I took a deep breath then blew it out. "The half Fae said that her parents made a deal with a dark

Fae. They get money basically, he gets her when she's old enough." I swallowed hard. The thought of what they wanted her for turned my stomach. If we hadn't found out, my girl would be wasting away in a dark Fae prison where he'd feed off her dark magic like a fucking battery supply. One that couldn't be recharged. "He wanted to feed off her dark magic."

Caleb nodded slowly. "They found a book in the main office and her name had a B next to it. They asked me what it was but I couldn't tell them. It stands for Betrothed. Not all the girls were but the camp was a way for shadow coven parents to pay debts they owed various... people." There was nothing else to call them especially if they weren't all Fae. "The contract is nearly unbreakable."

"Nearly? So there's a way?"

His jaw flexed then he nodded. "If you kill one of the parties that made the deal, it breaks. But the dark Fae won't be easy to kill."

"Her parents would be." Our eyes locked and it felt like we were making a pact. At the first chance we got, one of us would be killing Hazel's parents.

"It'd undo her binding as well. But the tricky part is, if the dark Fae they made the deal with kills her parents first, the contract is still binding. Then the only option is to kill him."

"Which is damn near impossible."

"Exactly." He moved closer. "Look, I don't mind being the bad guy because I am the bad guy. I'll take them out happily if they find him."

He, for some reason, was willing to take on killing two people so I wouldn't have to. "I promise you, when we find them, killing them won't be a problem for me. I won't hesitate but whoever gets there first needs to do it."

"Agreed."

I wet my lips because there was one more thing I needed to ask of him. "Can you not tell Hazel. I'll do it but..."

"You want it to be the right time and want to make sure she doesn't take on the guilt?"

"Exactly."

"Don't worry. I couldn't tell her about the betrothal if I wanted to. I'm bound to only speak of that with those that already know. As for her parents... I wouldn't do that."

I reach a hand out and he took it like we'd just made a pact or something.

In a way, we had.

We'd made a pact to kill the parents of the woman I loved.

No matter the cost.

18

HAZEL

It was warm and comfortable in Miller's bed. His heavy arm and thick leg were thrown over me, pulling me to his chest making the idea of getting out of this cocoon really unappealing. His breath feathered across the top of my head as my back pressed against his bare chest.

If I'd been worried about what his parents thought about us sleeping together, they'd proven there'd been no need.

Last night, Miller had taken Caleb up to his apartment then pulled me off to bed. Worked for me. I was dead on my feet by then and I'd nodded off almost as soon as we'd climbed into bed.

Now I could smell bacon wafting through the house and there would be no going back to bed.

They hadn't starved us at the camp, and it'd only been a few days, but I'd been cautious about eating anything there. Who knew what they put in it.

Potions to take away our free will?

I didn't know if that was possible but I wouldn't have put anything past the shadow coven and those that ran the camp. So I hadn't eaten much.

It took some careful movements to slip out from under Miller's arm without waking him up. He had looked more worn out than I had been and I had the sneaking suspicion that he hadn't slept much while I was gone.

After kissing his cheek carefully, I stopped at the bathroom to grabbed the toiletries bag that I'd put together at my house, stopped at the bathroom to brush my teeth then headed toward the kitchen. I'd also grabbed extra toothbrushes because my mom kept them stocked like a dentist. This way, no matter what happened, everyone would have fresh breath.

Having never met his parents before now, I would've thought I'd be more uncomfortable roaming around the house without Miller beside me. But he'd made it clear to them with his actions that I was his which meant, according to him, I was part of the family.

"It smells so good down here," I said once I'd entered the kitchen.

Eden glanced up from the snapping bacon with a smile. "I thought everyone would be starving this morning."

The closer I got to the bacon the louder my stomach became. "What can I help you with?" Though she looked like she had everything under control.

"You don't have to do anything." She flipped two pancakes, I swear, without looking.

"I'd like to help. You're helping me so much."

Eden turned to me with kind eyes and a soft smile. "Of course we'd help you, Hazel. Even if my son wasn't hopelessly in love with you. That's what the coven does."

But based on some things that Miller said, I didn't think that was what all of the coven did. Or at least if they did, then where were they?

"OK." She slapped her hands together and rubbed them. "If you insist, I could use help getting plates, silverware, and glasses out. We can set it up on the island, they can fill a plate then go to the table. Makes it easier on all of us."

"I can do that."

"When you're done, you could start the toast if you'd like."

She might've been humoring me but at least I was being useful. As she loaded serving plates up, she kept making the pancakes. In my world, I would've had to put the pancakes in the oven but every once in a while, Eden would hover her hands over them for a few seconds and steam billowed out again. Magical heat. Who knew?

"You're so hungry," she said suddenly bringing my eyebrows down. "I can hear your stomach from over here. Make yourself a plate."

"I can wait for—"

"Go ahead, Hazel. We have food whenever someone shows up. You can sit here at the island while I finish up. Keep me company."

"Thank you," I said quietly then grabbed a plate. I put a couple of pieces of bacon, two pancakes and a scoop of eggs on it. Though I wasn't sure I'd eat all it, I was hungry.

That was where Miller found me two minutes later when he came into the room. I had a strip of bacon in my fingers and in my mouth.

"There you are," he said as if he'd been looking everywhere for me. Miller was still in his pajama bottoms and no shit. My gaze slid down his smooth chest making me really wish he'd put on a shirt before coming down here. "I woke up and you were gone."

"The smell of bacon couldn't be ignored."

"Bacon is more a draw than my big warm bed?" He raised an eyebrow as my cheeks pinked up. Him saying that in front of his mother made me worry even when I knew it shouldn't have.

"Absolutely."

His mother snickered but kept her back turned to us. Miller leaned in to press his lips against mine. His hand clutched my chin to hold me in place as he lingered. But his mother was right freaking there.

Finally, he pulled back. "Mmm. You're right. Bacon is better."

His mother spun around and swatted at him with the spatula. Didn't actually hit him since he was too far away but she tried. "Would you let the girl eat?"

"Can't help it, Mom," he said before kissing her on the side of the head.

Within minutes everyone else joined us. Nellie and Gia looked well-rested and much more comfortable than they did yesterday. Cooper, Oliver, and Luken came having already gotten dressed while the girls and I were still in my pajamas. Only Miller wasn't ready for the day besides us. Caleb joined us moments later.

"Everything is ready. Just make a plate and let's go to the table.

I grabbed my plate and glass of orange juice and headed for the dining room so that I'd be out of the way. One by one, they all followed in. Gia and Nellie were right across from me, Miller on one side of me, Luken on the other, and Oliver next to the girls. Miller's parents were on the end together and Calen on the other side.

I'd noticed that whenever we sat down, if the girls weren't with me, or even if we were just standing, Miller was on one side and Luken on the other like they'd planned it.

Now, I didn't know Luken super well but given his friendship with Miller and how they'd been going all the way back to high school, it wasn't a stretch to think that Luken had agreed to be there to protect me if for some reason Miller couldn't.

"So what's the plan for today?" Cooper asked before he took a bite.

I was almost done by this time but I pushed the leftover pancake around my plate.

"Danna says she needs to talk to us," Luken told

me, though I didn't know why she always went through him.

"Who's Danna?" Caleb asked as he chewed whatever he'd just taken a bit of.

"She's on our council. She's been working with us. She's also the one that got Hazel's note to me." Miller took a drink of his juice.

"Ah."

"Wait." Miller turned toward Caleb. "Were you the one to deliver that?" He nodded which Miller snorted at and I didn't understand why. "You scared the shit out of her."

Caleb furrowed his brows. "I don't see how. I gave her the note then put as much distance between us as I could where she could still hear me."

"Yeah," Oliver started. "I think it was more a strange man coming up to her at her door at night kind of thing."

"Ah." He nodded. "That could do it."

"But," Luken interjected. "And no offense Caleb, she can't come here if there's a shadow coven member here."

"He left," I said because I didn't want him going out on a limb for me to get him ostracized.

"Yeah but she's on our counsel. She can't really be seen with a dark witch."

"I understand." Caleb pushed his plate away from himself then sat back with his arms over his chest.

"I don't." To me, it didn't make sense. "He left to help us. Why can't he stay."

Miller turned to me. "It's just for right now. We're trying to figure out who in our coven has been feeding shit to the shadow coven. She's getting us that information so if anyone saw her with a dark witch, they'd think it's her."

"Don't worry about it, Hazel," Caleb said but under his don't give a shit attitude, I thought I heard something else. Right now, I wouldn't make a big deal out of it.

Then he took his gaze over to Miller and raised an eyebrow. It was like they were having an unspoken conversation. Must not have gone Miller's way because he sighed.

"There is something I should share with you all. To keep you all in the loop." He shifted in his seat and raised a chin at his dad. It was like there was a language that I didn't understand between them and it was irritating. "Dad and I found some things out when we went to see Carina." Before I could ask, he turned to me. "She's a half Fae, half witch who gave us the Fae blood."

"She did have a lot of information," Cooper added and suddenly, everyone was done with breakfast.

"It was about the deal your parents made." Now he turned fully in his seat so that he was facing me like we were the only two people in the world in this conversation and not surrounded by seven other people.

"What deal?" I asked quietly because it didn't take being a witch to understand that I wasn't going to like what he was about to say.

"They made a deal with a dark Fae for them to get rich, basically. In exchange for something else."

"What?"

"You." I gasped. That was not what I'd expected at all. I expected it to be shitty but they were going to give me to someone else? I didn't understand. "The deal was for you, once you were old enough and I guess nineteen was that age, that you'd turn to dark magic, pledge the shadow coven, then... be married off to the dark Fae."

"Married... off?" I wasn't sure how to respond to that. "Why?"

"So that he could siphon off your dark magic little by little to boost his own."

The color drained from my face. I felt it and my

stomach churned with disgust. I was almost married off to a dark Fae? I might not have known what it fully meant but it was clear that it wasn't good.

"So what happens now?" This time I looked at Caleb for the answer.

He sighed then leaned his elbows on the table and folded his hands in front of his face. "To breath the contract, your parents of the Fae who made the deal have to die. Fae are notoriously hard to kill so…"

I spun my head back to Miller. "You're going to kill my parents?"

"It's the only way. It'll release you from their binding as well."

I swallowed hard. "I hate them. I wanted away from them. I never wanted them dead."

"Doesn't sound like we have a choice," Oliver told me and it seemed that everyone was automatically in agreement.

Well shit.

"I don't know how to respond to that," I told him honestly.

"You don't have to."

"Does that mean that our parents made some deal that involved us?" Gia asked. "Is that what the camp was about?"

Caleb adjusted his weight like he was uncomfortable with the answer. "Yes." At least he was truthful. "You both are payment for a contract."

"For what?" Nellies asked but Caleb shook his head.

"I can't tell you. I wish I could."

"You're bound on that one too?" I asked to which he nodded so I told them, "He can only discuss it with someone who already knows."

Gia dropped roughly back into her chair. "Well, that sucks."

Yes. Yes it did.

"Danna's just a minute away," Luken said as he slid his phone over the table.

"I'll go back to the apartment." Caleb pushed from his chair then gave me one last look before heading out the back.

"I'm going to get this all cleared away," Eden told us but we all stood to help clear the table and quickly put things in the sink. The dishes would have to wait.

"Is there a spell that would clean your dishes?" I asked as we headed back out to the dining room.

She giggled but shook her head. "Not one I know of but you could always work on creating one yourself."

"That sucks. I'd use that one all the time."

She patted my arm before moving back to her seat.

Luken came back in with a woman just a few inches taller than me who had her long, dark brown hair hanging over her shoulder in a thick braid. She was wearing shorts and a T-shirt looking like she was headed to a baseball game or something. Not what I would've imagined someone on the coven counsel to look like.

"Nellie, Gia, Hazel, this is Danna Payne," Luken introduced her which made me roll my eyes.

After greeting her, I turned to him. "You know we all went to the same high school, right? I know who she is."

He held his hands up in defeat and smirked. "How was I supposed to know you remembered."

"What's going on?" Miller butt in. Clearly he wanted to get this things going.

"OK." She took the first chair she'd come to and it happened to be the one Luken had previously sat in next to me. "We are now sure that there is a high level leak in our coven. At first, as you boys know we were thinking it was just one of the witches. But as we dug deeper and the person is on our counsel. Now, you know it's not me. There are some suspicions but we have to be sure before doing anything. If not... catastrophe."

"What can we do about Caleb?" I asked interrupting their very important coven business. "He's marked because he was a dark witch. If he doesn't want to be anymore?"

"There's a process for that," Miller explained though I noticed that he'd put clothes on. It must've been when I was in the kitchen cleaning up and I hadn't realized until right now.

Somehow I felt better about him wearing jeans and a T-shirt now that others were around than I would've with him still bare-chested. I didn't know his history with Danna and I didn't want to.

"If nothing more, in the short term," Danna added. "We could block his dark magic. It'd take me a bit to make the potion but we could do that until we get this shit figured out."

Luken shook his head. "We might need his dark magic."

"OK, well, a problem for a different time."

Though I had no idea why they'd need Caleb's dark magic and was slightly uncomfortable with the way they were talking about him as if he was something for us to use and not a person who'd become my friend.

"Right," I said. Sorry.

I went to step back but Miller grabbed my arm, slid his hand down until he could wrap his fingers around mine then gently pulled me back close.

Danna set a large envelope on the table then opened it. There were papers in there which I didn't understand. Everything was digital now.

"These are copies of some things I've found. I tried to just take pictures because that was quicker but you could really make anything out."

Ah, yes. That would explain it.

"Oh my god." Nellie stepped back, holding onto Gia's hand tightly and I didn't know what had struck fear into them.

I leaned over to look at what they had and I saw it. There was a copy of a photograph, while grainy, I recognized the man right away.

"Who is that?" I asked pointing at the man I knew had icy blue eyes. For some reason, that man's eyes wigged me out but Miller's never did. Maybe it was the intent behind them.

Miller leaned over to look. "That's Michael. He's the head of our counsel."

Danna flipped through a couple of pages and spoke without looking up at us. "I copied that one because the guy in it used to be a member of our coven but no one really knows what happened to him. He *said* he was moving out of Echo Valley but no one really knows so that's suspicious. Another member thought he might've defected. I thought he might be important." Now she looked up at me with light brown eyes. "Do you know who he is?"

I shook my head and wet my lips. "No. I don't know who he is. But I do know who he is." I kept pointing at the one they'd told me was called Michael. Though I'd never met or seen him in Echo Valley.

"How do you know him, Hazel?" Miller asked gently.

"He was at the camp." I cleared my throat. "He was the director of the camp or whatever. The one who gave the orders. He was there the night I was brought in."

Miller's jaw hardened. "Are you telling me that the head of our counsel is working with the shadow coven?"

"I don't know," I told him honestly. "But I think he's the head of the shadow coven."

19

MILLER

THE HEAD of our coven counsel was playing double agent? He was there the night Hazel was brought in?

If he's the one that took her or hurt her, I was going to kill him with my bare hands.

"How can that be?" Mom asked.

Gia and Nellie got freaked out by all of this so they said they were going up to their room. Hazel had told me that they'd been at the camp a few days longer than her so who knew what they witnessed.

"Yeah, how could Michael be working with the dark coven?" Oliver added.

Dad agreed. "Yeah, he's been here twenty years."

"Guys," Danna said as she pushed out of her chair. "This is new information for me too. Hang on." She leaned on her hands on the table toward Hazel. "Are you sure you saw him?"

She nodded and squeezed my hand tighter. "He was there. I mostly remembered him because people seemed to fall all over themselves when he was around." I swallowed hard. "Also he had these scary, icy blue eyes. Reminded me of yours except for the scary part. His were unsettling. Yours never have been."

My eyebrows were slammed down as I flexed the muscle in my jaw and then released it. "So Michael?" I directed that at Danna.

"I... I don't know but..." She blew out a rough breath. "It would make sense. Remember when I told you that we'd convinced Michael to not read people's minds because it wasn't right?" I nodded. "He didn't agree. At all." She swallowed roughly. "Another member and I reached out to Serena Good. She helped us with a potion that would block him."

"How would that help anyone else?" Dad asked her.

"We've been dumping it into the water supply. I won't tell you who helped me because it's one thing to put my neck on the line but another to choose that for someone else."

"You've been drugging us?" Luken's body was tense.

She sighed. "Yes, but it was for the greater good. Michael was adamant that the only way he could keep things under control was if he could hear everything everyone was thinking. It was a violation. But his insistence was what had me start questioning everything."

Silence hung in the air. Hazel might not have been following all of this because she hadn't been here as long but she listened and tried to make sense of it all.

Hazel took a breath then asked, "Shouldn't we ask Caleb about him? About this?"

Danna took a step back. "Yes. You should. But I can't be here for it. I'll leave everything but someone's going to need to fill me in."

"We got you," Oliver assured her before she hurried out of the house.

I released Hazel's hand then moved around her as I headed toward the kitchen. A moment later, the kitchen door shut behind me.

I took the stairs to my apartment two at a time then pounded on the door. Caleb opened it like he'd been close already.

"We need you inside," I told him.

He nodded and stepped outside. "Is the council witch still there?"

"No." I started down the steps with him behind me. "She left so that we could bring you in. We've got some questions."

"I see." He took a hit off the potion Mom had given him so he could step through the back door with me.

As we got back to the dining room, Mom looked up at Dad with big eyes and asked, "Could he really have been here for so long without us knowing?"

Yeah. Apparently he fucking could have been.

Dad folded his arms over his chest. "I don't know. You'd think Serena would've fully vetted him. She wouldn't have let a dark witch on the council."

"What if he isn't?" Luken asked which got him questioning looks. "What if he isn't a dark witch? Or not fully anyway. We don't know a lot about the dark magic so maybe there are spells that block others from knowing or something."

"What about the Fae blood?" Hazel asked which brought all of their attention to her causing her to shift uncomfortably. "I realize I don't know a lot about this stuff but if the Fae blood potion blocks Caleb's dark magic so he can get into the house right now, couldn't Michael do something similar? Maybe there's a bigger spell that doesn't just block it from a ward but from everyone."

Oliver scratched over his stubbled chin. "Shit. Yeah. That's possible. It'd take a fuck ton of Fae blood though."

"Or maybe it's not Fae blood," Luken offered. "I mean there's Fae blood, he could've made a deal with a demon—"

"Demon?" Hazel squeaked. The more she discovered about this world the more I worried she'd even want to be a part of it. Hearing that the things nightmares were made of really existed could be scary at hell.

"Yeah." Luken adjusted his weight as if he just realized I was in the room and had no idea what he was talking about. "They aren't around much but it's not impossible that he found one and made a deal. For what, I wouldn't know."

There were so many questions on the tip of my girl's tongue, I could see them but I'd answer them later.

"This guy." I snagged the picture off the table and pointed to Michael. It wasn't a great picture but clear enough.

"Yeah," Calen hugged. "That's Michael. I wouldn't call him the head of our coven—or the shadow coven—but he's a decision-maker. More of the planner. The architect might be a better word. He's the one that maps out the agenda."

This all sounded like we were talking about some board meeting and not people's lives.

"The camp was his idea years ago. He thought that if dark witches couldn't convince their own kids that the camp would be able to do it."

"Fuck," I muttered. "He's been the head of our council since Serena Good left after the death of her daughter."

"So he's been playing both sides." It was a statement. Not a question. "I mean it was a good plan."

"The fuck are you saying?" Luken began toward Caleb while Hazel slithered closer to my parents where I was happy to have her.

"What?" Caleb asked after not having moved. He didn't even take his hand out of his pocket as Luken came angrily toward him. "You have to admit that being on the council of a light coven would be a pretty easy way to funnel new witches over to the shadow coven."

"Yeah, but he's fucking with our lives."

Caleb shook his head. "I didn't say I agreed with it. Just that it's kind of genius."

"If Michael is really a dark witch, why in the hell

would he send me to train Hazel as a light witch?" I glanced over at Hazel but then focused on my father.

But it was Luken who had an idea. "If he could read all of your thoughts, he would've known how you felt about her way back in high school."

I didn't care who knew how I felt about Hazel. More than that I wanted them to know. She was here and wasn't going anywhere unless she decided. But fuck I hoped none of this would scare her away.

If she left Echo Valley or rejected our coven, I'd have a serious decision to make. But who was I kidding? There wasn't a decision. Wherever Hazel went, I'd be with her. She just needed to realize what the life of a covenless witch would entail.

We would be unprotected. But I was getting way ahead of myself.

"Yeah, but why would he want her trained as a light witch?" A smile played on Hazel's lips over me having no qualms about everyone knowing my feelings for her. But I didn't have any. They all knew I loved her already, most knew I loved her then. This was just how it was going to be.

"He'd want you to come with her," Caleb offered. I turned to him with his brows furrowed wanting more of an explanation. "Think about it. If he knew you were in love with her and he had you spending time with her, he probably figured she'd fall for you."

"That's quite the assumption." Hazel's words came out pretty low like she meant to say it in her head and she was met with a round of low chuckles. Her cheek turned a light pink which showed she hadn't meant for any of us to hear it.

"Baby." I turned toward her, a smile playing on my lips. "There was never any doubt."

I shook my head then waved my finger in the air to get Caleb to continue.

There was the sound of humor in his voice when he continued. "So, if you began training her, you'd be getting her ready to go to the camp. But feelings would've grown so when she decided to pledge the shadow coven, he probably figured you'd convert to be with her."

"That is quite the detailed plan," Oliver said then blew out a breath. "Where he failed was in wanting her to be a virgin. Sending Miller, who'd been in love with her for years, put that at risk."

Hazel's cheeks burned brighter over us discussing her virginity or lack thereof in front of everyone including her boyfriend's parents. The look on her face told me that she wished the ground would open up and suck her down.

Caleb shook his head. "Michael wouldn't have cared about that. That was for the deal her parents made. Why would he give two shits about it? If they didn't fulfill the contract, the Fae would've taken care of them. It wouldn't have hurt the shadow coven because it wasn't a coven agreement. So yeah, he'd lose her parents but he'd gain her, you, and any future children. It was a net gain."

That was... a lot to take in.

"Plus," Caleb continued and cross his arms over his chest. "He seemed hell-bent on getting you specifically into the coven."

He wanted me? I glanced at my parents who were clearly surprised by this new information. Mom pushed out of the chair and stood in front of Dad.

"Why?" she asked but Caleb shook his head.

"I don't know. He never said but Miller's name came up quite a few times." He took a drink from the glass of water on the table. I don't even remember whose that was. "Did he have a connection to Miller? Like when he joined? Was Miller more powerful than he should've been? Anything like that?"

Mom's face paled then she stumbled back into her chair and sat with a thud, holding her head in her hands. My chest filled with anxiety... and the knowledge that no one was going to like the answer.

"He showed up the day Miller was born," Dad began. "We were at a cabin for her safety. Once we found out she was pregnant from Beltane and..." He swallowed hard. "Other girls had disappeared, I wanted to keep her safe. The day Miller was born, a dark witch showed up. Michael came out of nowhere and killed the witch. Then he came here with us."

"That would be a net gain," Caleb told them. "Kill one witch. Gain three."

"He didn't gain us," I snapped.

"I know but that's not how he would've been thinking."

"How did he show up there?" Now it was Luken.

Everyone was standing in a sort of circle at one end of the table. Except for Mom who was still holding her head and had become very quiet.

"How did he show up at the cabin?" Luken asked again. "Serena would've had it warded to hell and back."

A small sob came from Mom causing Dad to put his hand on her shoulder and rub it comfortingly. Hazel went to her, wrapped her arm around my mom's shoulder and pulled her into a hug. Mom leaned her head on my girlfriend and patted her arm.

Then suddenly Mom pushed up, dried her eyes, and patted Hazel's cheek softly before standing. I followed her.

"There's only one way," she told us. "The only way Michael, a dark witch, could've found us was if blood was calling blood."

I froze.

Blood calling blood?

Michael wasn't related to either of my parents which could've only meant one thing.

"Fuck," Luken muttered from beside me. He'd put it together too.

If his blood was calling his blood, there was only one person whose blood he could've been calling out to.

"What does that mean?" Hazel slipped her hand in mine which I took and squeezed.

I turned to her and ran my thumb over her cheek. "That means Michael was the one who raped my mother at Beltane." I swallowed hard. "My eyes aren't a fucking genetic anomaly. They're an inherited trait."

Hazel's eyes widened and her mouth formed a soft O. All I was filled with was anger.

And the need to break Michael's neck.

When I turned back, my father hand my mom wrapped tightly in his arms. "He's been here the whole time," she said against his chest. "We didn't even know it."

Mom had made peace with what happened to her a long time ago. Or so I was told. But finding out that the man who raped, impregnated, and tried to kidnap you had been living so close this whole time probably brought everything right back to the surface.

It was enough that every fucking time she looked at me, she would've been reminded of that night and what she didn't remember happening to her.

How had she lived like that? How in the hell could she have looked at me every day of my fucking life knowing how I came to be.

Acid burned my throat and I swallowed it down. When I glanced around, Luken, Oliver, and Caleb weren't in the room. Like they knew this was personal and wanted to give us some space. But I held on to Hazel with everything I had.

"Don't," Mom choked out as she stepped from Dad's arms. The anger on his face was palpable but I didn't know if I was feeling his or mine or both.

Probably both.

Mom came to me and took my face in her hands. Still, I didn't let go of Hazel. I needed her close.

"Don't think the thoughts you're thinking," she told me.

I forced a grin for her sake. "Are you saying you can read minds now?"

"I don't have to." Her watery eyes searched mine. "This has nothing to do with you, Miller." Well, it had a little to do with me. "What he did doesn't change anything. I love you. Your dad loves you. There was never any question about you or that. I wouldn't give you up to make all the other shit go away. You're my son. Not his. You're mine and your dad's."

How did she know what I'd been thinking? Easy answer. She'd known me every day of my fucking life.

"Don't go getting any ideas," Dad told me as he slapped my shoulder. "That fucker is mine."

I chuckled but there was no humor behind it. "We'll see who gets to him first."

Dad led Mom out of the room like he knew I needed a minute with my girl. I wrapped her up in my arms and held tightly.

"Are you OK?" Her voice muffled against my chest.

I kissed the top of her head and said, "No. But I will be."

She didn't know that I planned to murder Michael with my bare hands, no magic needed. The only problem was, I had no doubt that my dad had the same plan.

It would only come down to who got to him first.

20

HAZEL

THERE WERE times in my life that I wished I was a fly on the wall to overhear conversations.

This wasn't one of those times.

First, I was in the room hearing the things live already. Second, this information was so personal that I was a bit uneasy being there in the first place. Yet, I wanted to be whatever Miller needed me to be.

He'd just found out that the man his entire coven had trusted for decades was really a dark witch who had roofied and impregnated his mother. The anger that rolled off him had me worried for everyone but mostly him.

Miller would want revenge, which was a normal response. But how would he deal with the aftermath of killing that man? Probably fine, I'd guess given that I knew he'd had to do it before.

What a strange turn my life had taken.

Miller still had me wrapped in his arms, his chin leaning on my head. I held him as tightly as I could. He said he was going to be OK but I wasn't sure I believed him.

"You sure?" I asked after I put just enough space between the two of us so that he could still be holding me but I could look into his eyes.

"Yeah." He sighed then dropped into the nearest chair and brought me with him. One of my legs was on the outside of each of his so that I was facing him. "Yeah. I'm sure I'll be OK. Just have to get my hands on a certain witch."

In any other situation, I'd feel bad for the witch in question having both Miller and Cooper gunning for him. In this case, not at all. After the things he did, he deserved whatever he got and I didn't even know the full extent of Miller and Cooper's powers but what I had seen should've sent the witch running.

Miller's hands settled on my thighs, heating the skin that my shorts didn't cover.

"That could've been you," he said quietly.

"What?" I brought my hands to his cheeks and

ran my thumbs over his skin. "What do you mean that could've been me?"

He swallowed hard, his clear blue eyes settling on mine. "What they did to my mom… they could've done that to you at that fucking camp. All because I was too busy getting you in bed to recharge that fucking amulet."

On instinct, my fingers went to where the amulet used to lay on my chest. I'd grown so used to checking for it that I hate to not have it.

"They took it," I told him quietly.

"I know." He sighed. "We found it in a field when we were scrying for you."

I allowed myself a tiny grin. "If I remember correctly, though, what we were doing instead of charging the amulet was pretty great."

He snorted but there was absolutely zero humor on his face. "Still wasn't worth them getting their fucking hands on you."

It was guilt. He was blaming himself and that was the last thing any of us needed.

"Miller." I gave him a gentle kiss. "It's not your fault."

"The fuck it isn't. I was supposed to protect you and they still fucking got you."

"You came to get me," I countered. "I think you've

done your job. Listen." I adjusted myself slightly closer to him. "I'm fine. Nellie, Gia... we're fine. You got to us in time. None of the other shit matters."

His jaw tensed as he shook his head slightly. Didn't look like I was going to convince him that he wasn't to blame any time soon.

"I should go see if my mom's OK," he finally said but made no effort to move me off him. "You can come with me."

Uh... no. That seemed like a wholly personal conversation that I shouldn't be a part of. If Miller needed me there, that would've been different but he already heard all of the bad news, I hoped, and right now, it should just be the three of them.

"If you need me to, I'll come with you. But I think you should talk to your mom and dad alone. Your mom is probably in a deeply personal place right now. I know I would be." He tensed. Maybe that wasn't a thought I should've put in his head right now.

"Yeah." he sighed as he ran a hand down the side of my head. "Maybe your right. What are you going to do?"

"I'm going to check on Nellie and Gia."

He nodded, kissed me like we wouldn't see each other for days, then slid me off his lap. Miller held my hand until we got to the stairs and watched me as I climbed. His eyes were like a caress over my skin as I made it up the stairs.

I hurried up the until I could slip into the room where I knew Nellie and Gia were staying. When I opened the door without knocking, Nellie was sitting on the bed with her back against the head-board and her legs stretched out in front of her while Gia was in the chair at the desk slowly swinging from left to right like a bored kid waiting for her parents to be finished with their grown-up conversation.

"You two all right?" I asked when they both glanced up at the sound of the door opening.

"We're fine," Gia told me and stopped her swinging. "it was just getting to be a lot down there."

"Yeah. It as." I flopped onto my stomach across the foot of the bed. "It's so weird," I told them. "I didn't even know witches existed until recently now there are dark witches, light witches, Fae, Demons... I feel like I'm in bizarro world."

Gia sat up straight. "I'm sorry. Demons?"

I snorted. "Thank you. It's weird right. But Luken said that maybe Michael made a deal with one... How could our parents think it was a good idea to allow us to be so uninformed."

"I grew up knowing about the shadow coven and dark witches," Gia explained. "My parents didn't bind me… or at least not like that. I knew what they did. But what worked against them was that I didn't like what I knew. I didn't want to hurt people… be part of a group that could do those things."

"My parents bound my power," Nellie told us. "But they didn't stop me from knowing that I'm a witch and what would be expected of me one day. They just didn't want me to have the powers to explore anything else." She took a deep breath. "You know I heard of some of the things the shadow coven has done and there's no world where I'd want to be a part of it."

"Like what?" I asked. Sure, I knew some of the things but not everything. Probably not even enough to scratch the surface.

"Like wipe out an entire light coven. Killed the women and children too." Nellie shivered then ran her hands up her arms like she was cold. "I couldn't imagine being OK with killing a baby like that. I'm fully pro-choice but not like that."

"Seriously?" I asked. That seemed too heinous even for the bad guys.

"Yeah," Gia confirmed. "I was like seven when they did that. But it's other stuff too. I overheard my parents once talking about the new members they'd created. It was a weird way to say it so I kept listening. Apparently, they infiltrated a coven's Beltane celebration, roofied some of the young women's punch and raped them. Then they came back and took those who were pregnant so that the babies could be raised as dark witches."

"That's..." My heart ached for the women, like Eden, who went through that. I couldn't imagine and hoped that I'd never have to find out what it was like to go through something like that. It wasn't my story to tell so I didn't offer up what I knew about Miller's mom. "Wait. But the moms they took were light witches... what'd they do to the moms?"

Gia shook her head. "That I didn't hear other than they figured the moms would change teams to stay with their babies. Either way, they weren't leaving with babies."

"What if they didn't stay with the baby?"

She shrugged. "I don't know but I can't imagine that they allowed those witches to return to their coven."

My stomach twisted painfully. "I think I'm going to be sick." Then I dropped my head back to the bed and tried to block out all the terrible things that I'd just learned might've been in store for me if Miller hadn't gotten there in time.

"Miller feels guilty," I told them quietly. "About me being taken."

Nellie nodded slowly. "It makes sense."

Yeah, it did. Doesn't mean I liked it.

"He loves you," Gia added. "Of course he'd feel like he didn't do enough to protect you. You were taken to the camp after all."

"Yeah but it was my fault really. I insisted I had to go home to get some clothes. He wanted to come with me but I didn't want to fuck up his life. He had to work."

Nellie nudged my shoulder with her foot. "Next time let the man go with you. I'm one hundred percent sure that he'd put himself between you and a bullet."

That was exactly what I was afraid of.

Miller getting hurt or worse all because of me. From this point forward, or really since the moment those men grabbed me, I wouldn't push back at him for the sake of his job or my stubborn independence. That didn't mean he'd tell me what to do just that I'd look at things from his side first.

"What are we going to now?" Gia asked. "It's not

like we can stay at Miller's parents the rest of our lives."

"What do you want to do?"

"Join a light coven ASAP." Gia didn't have to think about that too hard and Nellie agreed. "It'll offer some protection against the shadow coven. Give me people to have my back when the shit hits the fan."

"I'll have your back," I told her then thought of a caveat. "Once I know what the fuck I'm doing."

The three of us giggled like we weren't in the mess we were in. We had escaped the shadow coven and they probably wouldn't stop until they got us given that deals had been made with us as the payment.

"I wonder what my deal was," Nellie said then glanced up at us. "Is that weird?"

"No." Because I'd thought the same thing. "I've been wondering if all of our deals were the same or what other fucked up plan one of our parents had."

A light knock on the door brought our conversation to a halt. When the door creaked open, Miller stuck his head through.

"You three all right?" he asked while glancing at each of us.

"We're good. Are you?"

He nodded sadly. "Hazel. Your parents are at the front door."

My eyebrows slammed down in confusion. "What? They're here? You know if they—"

He held up a hand. "They can't get in. They can't get to you. But I wanted to check to see if you wanted to see them before I use an energy ball to zap them to Siberia."

"See them? Why would I..." I let that trail off as I searched Miller's eyes for understanding. No way would he want me around my parents yet here he was saying that I could talk to them. There had to be a reason....

That's when I remembered that the only way to break the contract was to kill my parents. He was asking me because this was going to be the last chance I had. For all I knew, he was going to kill them right there on the front porch.

He pulled his whole body through the doorway, now standing tall in the room. "I'm not going to kill them on the front porch." He ran a hand over his face. "Actually, I can't kill them on the front porch otherwise I absolutely would."

"Why can't you?" Gia asked the question we all had to be thinking .

"It's a thing with the coven. They have it spelled

so we can't kill another witch in town. That way the humans don't freak out."

"Huh." I bobbed my head like I understood any of this. "Caleb would've appreciated that information when he brought my note. Pretty sure he thought he was going to get fried."

He snorted. "Danna would've done it too, I think. She doesn't usually fuck around but yeah... Unless we're attacked, I can't do shit. Which really pisses me off right now."

Nellie nudged me with her foot again. "See? You and a bullet."

I shook my head as Miller's brows furrowed in confusion. I'd explain later.

"Anyway, do you want to talk to these pieces of shit or can I get a little satisfaction right now?"

Fighting back a laugh, I told him, "I think I should see them. See if they'll give me some answers."

"Then I can zap them?"

I pushed up off the bed. "Then you can zap away."

Hurrying down the steps, I had Nellie and Gia on my heels. They likely wouldn't get answers from their parents ever so this was of interest to them if for no other reason than to see if my parent's logic could apply to them.

Miller's face was dark and menacing as he marched toward the front door. Then he stepped aside so that I could face the people who effectively sold me to a dark Fae. Whatever that meant. I still didn't understand it all.

"Don't open the front door," he told me quietly. "The spell works either way but I want something between you and them."

"Got it."

Then I was facing the people who were supposed to love and support me but had done neither.

"Why are you here?" I asked them. "You have to know that it's a bad idea. There are people here who want you dead."

My dad gave me a wicked grin. "We know they can't kill us in town."

"Unless provoked," I countered. "You being here seems like a provocation."

Dad's smile faltered for a moment. "We haven't done anything."

"Have done anything?" I yelled suddenly aware that Miller, Nellie, and Gia weren't the only people in the room with me. Everyone else had filed in either to watch my family drama or more likely to be there in case this shit went south. "You fucking sold me to a dark Fae to use as his power supply. I feel like you've done something."

"He won't hurt you," Mom assured me but her assurances were shit. Neither of them could be trusted at all. But if we don't deliver baby, he's going to kill us. Without us, there will be no one looking after you once you've married him."

I gagged while Miller's body stiffened. He wasn't able to see my parents because he had his back against the wall next to the door watching me. He really didn't like what they had to say and opened his mouth to counter but I shook my head. I'd handle my parents.

"You wouldn't have been looking out for me either way. You made the deal. What happens to you if it isn't my problem. Right now, I'm hoping I can help take care of the people that I love." I held my arms out to indicate everyone in this house.

Caleb caught the corner of my eye as he quietly slid in next to Miller and whispered something I could hear. Something Miller shook his head at.

Oh shit.

Caleb wasn't a light witch. Did that mean the spelling the light coven had done wouldn't apply to him? Just another time I wish I understood how all of this worked.

"You're so selfish." Dad shook his head as he took a step forward causing me to take a small step back even though Miller assured me that the ward on the door was solid and I knew that there were at least six people in this room that wouldn't let my parents touch me.

"I'm selfish?" Tears burned my eyes but I didn't know why. Maybe I was going to mourn the childhood I could've had. The life I never got. The one where my parents were doing something other than raising me like a pig to slaughter. "You gave up your child for what? Money? Power? Success?" I shook my head with disdain. "No. I'm pretty sure you're the selfish one."

Dad continued as if he hadn't heard me. "We weren't even supposed to have kids," he snapped. "We needed you to be a virgin. That way he would know that your magic was untouched. And if I would've known the one we did have would've turned into a little slut who spread her legs for the first light witch to show interest, I would've made a different deal."

Miller shot forward like a man out for blood and

he probably was but he didn't get the chance to whatever it was he'd planned. Dad got too close.

He stepped up to the door like he was going to rip it open and the ward glowed a bright blue hue as it covered him. His body shook like he was being electrocuted, his eyes rolled back in his head. He fell back several steps, sweating and breathing heavily like he'd just run a marathon.

Then the two of them disappeared.

When I say disappeared, I mean gone. They didn't walk away. They just vanished.

My heart pounded in my chest as my eyes burned from... fear, anger, and confusion. All of it rolled into one.

Miller had me in his arms, held tightly to his chest. "Don't listen to them," he told me, his mouth close to my ear. "They don't know you. They don't know that it took years for me to get you to spread your legs."

I snorted and a lot of the emotions that my parents had called up slipped away. There was also a low chuckle in the room from the guys which meant that they'd heard what he said. I couldn't be bothered to care.

"I'm going to make sure they can't hurt you again, Hazel. That's a promise."

Nodding, I couldn't speak right then. This was too much. Most girls got parents who at least didn't call them a slut. I got mine. Life really wasn't fair.

Before I could verbalize any of that, the floor vibrated under my feet, the house began to shake, then there was the loudest explosion I'd ever heard that caused us all to hurry for the front window and door. We didn't sit outside and Miller kept his arm around me.

A bright green plume of smoke rose from the other side of town. I'd never seen anything like that before. Most smoke was black, white, or gray. This was something else.

Luken was the first to speak. "What the fuck was that?"

No one seemed to know but it was for sure nothing good.

21

MILLER

THAT EXPLOSION CAME from across town near the council house. Since Echo Valley was a small town, that meant it was too fucking close.

"Oliver and I will go check it out," Luken said then the two of them pushed through the door. I should've been going with them but for the first time, I was fucking torn.

With Nellie, Gia, and most importantly Hazel here, I couldn't go. Sure, my dad and Caleb could've kept them safe but I couldn't bring myself to leave her. Maybe that made me a pussy but right now, all I knew was that the shadow coven would get Hazel back over my cold, dead body and I couldn't do that if I was across town trying to figure out what happened.

"It's the shadow coven," Caleb said sounding absolutely certain.

"How do you know?" I turned to him with my arms folded over my chest. I wanted to trust him because having him on our side would help keep Hazel safe but I didn't think I was totally there yet.

"Trust me. I know. I can feel the fucking pull." The level of disgust dripping from his words definitely helped convince me that he wouldn't be going back to the shadow coven on his own.

"Why do they care if my parents' debt is paid?" Hazel asked her voice wavering.

Caleb sighed. "I don't think they do. At this point, they're probably just pissed over what you all did at the camp." He shifted uncomfortably. "And probably looking for me. Which, I can go. Take a little of the heat off you all."

"No," mom said right away. "We're not leaving you out there on your own. You've helped us. We're going to help you. That's what we do."

I couldn't have agreed more. Besides, I was pretty sure Hazel would've protested even if I didn't agree. Somehow in that camp, those two became close. Close enough that in another situation I might've been suspicious but I knew Hazel. She'd never do anything like that and I trusted her implicitly.

"Where's my phone?" she asked as if she hadn't considered she had one until this moment. "I bet my parents could track it. Maybe that's how they knew I was here."

I ran a hand over her arm to reassure her. "It wouldn't take two guesses for them to figure out where I'd take you to protect you." I took a breath. "But we had to trash your phone specifically for that reason."

Her face feel and I understood. Most of the time, our entire lives are in our phones. Our memories were in there. "Hey." I pulled her close not caring who the fuck was watching. "I sent myself all of your pictures so once this bullshit is over, we get you a new phone and I can send them back to you."

She slapped a hand over her face. "All of them?"

I snorted. "Yeah. All of them. Not sure what you're embarrassed about, you're adorable in all of them."

She groaned and shook her head. "Just so no one thinks I had naked pictures of myself, I'm referring to some that a friend and I took of us being absolute idiots."

"Still adorable."

She groaned and pushed at my stomach while I tried not to laugh.

Those photos from her phone had helped get me through the days when she wasn't with me. Even the ones she's referring to. It looked like she and her friend were messing around and there were pics of them posing in some ridiculous ways but it was her having fun. I'd needed to see that and I had them for her.

She'd have her memories back.

Before we could delve into that any further, Oliver and Luken burst back into the room.

"We couldn't get close," Luken said out of breath.

"They attacked the counsel house which makes them fucking idiots," Oliver added. "That place is protected to hell and back but the light coven has come out to defend Echo Valley."

"That will keep the shadow coven busy for at least a little while." Luken moved further into the house with a purpose. I just didn't know what that purpose was. "Danna thinks we need to stash the girls and Caleb somewhere."

"Any ideas?" Oliver asked.

There was a pregnant pause before anyone spoke but when Mom did, she also took a step forward. "Cooper and I have a place."

"Yeah. That'd be perfect." Dad glanced around. "Girls, go pack some things," he told them. "Whatever you'll need for a while." Hazel squeezed my hand before the three of them hurried up the stairs to pack their clothes. "If you have time, pack a bag for Miller, too," he called after my girl. "The guys will get it all into the car."

"I can do that," I told him, not wanting to put it on Hazel.

"No, you won't have time." He moved through the house to the kitchen. "Eden, get them some food boxed up." Mom gave him a nod then got to work on the kitchen. The spell she cast had the cupboards flying open and bags coming out from under the sink. "Oliver, Luken, get to the potion room and take... well whatever you can fit. There's a crate in there and the satchel." Those two bolted off but dad called after, "Especially the potions already made."

"OK. What am I supposed to be doing?" I asked him. "What are you planning?"

Dad pulled the map that we'd been using to scry for Hazel out and flipped it around. Caleb was right there so this wasn't the case of him not wanting anyone else to know what he was about to tell me.

"The girls aren't leaving this house until everything is ready. Then they can but we're going to ward you to death." He looked up and called out, "Don't forget the Fae blood. Take it all."

"All?" I countered. That would mean they wouldn't be able to fortify the wards. "Explain."

"Here." His meaty finger landed on a specific spot on the map. One that didn't have anything on it. It wasn't a town, it was... nothing. He circles a spot off the main road. "Your mom and I bought a cabin years ago and kept it a secret from everyone. Not a single person knows it exits. Even the realtor died a year after we bought the place. It's not registered under our names and it's in the middle of the woods that we've let overgrow as much as possible." He took a breath. "On top of that, it's got rune wards all around it that keep the place hidden from humans and witches alike. And anyone inside the circle should be safe."

"You've had this the whole time?" I asked.

He nodded. "After what happened to your mother, I wanted somewhere I could send her and you to keep you safe if the shit really hit the fan."

"Why wouldn't you just move there?" Caleb asked. "If it's so safe."

Dad shook his head. "The runes only last so long. Once there are people there, the timer starts. We can't recharge it so the low-level magic keeps the place hidden along with the forest. No one goes out there. But to protect the people, it's much harder. We won't be able to recast them so it provides limited time protection. We didn't want to use it unless we had to."

"Why's it so hard?" Caleb again.

As part of the light coven, I knew about runes and the fact that there were only certain ways to cast them. Apparently, the shadow coven didn't want their witches to know it was even possible.

"It has to be cast in blood," I told him.

"We've all got blood."

"Not our blood," Dad said. "There are only three types of blood that will work and all are very hard to come by."

Caleb snorted. "I've done some shady shit in my life. I'm sure I can find what you need."

Dad shook his head as Oliver and Luken passed through the kitchen out to the cars. I assumed I'd be driving the girls and Caleb like I had been. Oliver would be in his and Luken either with him or on his bike.

"Doubtful," Dad countered. "You need angel blood, demon blood, or the blood of the original witch."

"Fuck," he huffed out. "Yeah, I guess that's a tall order."

Angels and demons existed but rarely came to our

world which meant you'd have to try to summon them and they fucking hated that shit. Usually, it didn't end well for the summoner. As for the original witch... well, that woman's been dead for hundreds of years.

"How'd you get the blood?" I asked him as Mom directed Luken and Oliver to load up the food.

"I'd rather not tell you that." Another explosion rocked the house only this time it sounded much closer. "But you're going here. It'll buy us some time with the protection. But once you're there, you're all going to get some wards up anyway. The ruins will stop the coven for a while but Fae can see through the shield. It's a kind of glamor. Anyway, your mom and I will head out there when we can given what's happening now and we'll bring more previsions. I don't know how long you'll be out there."

"There should be enough room for everyone though some of you will have to double up," Mom explained.

That was fine. I knew who I'd be double up with.

"Now you've got to get out of here." Dad handed me the map. "Those explosions are getting closer."

Dad came over to me and put a hand on each shoulder. "You go and you don't stop. No matter what."

"I know, Dad." That meant even if I saw our house go up in flames, I'm to get the fuck out of there and not turn back for them.

That might be easier said than done. These were my parents but I had to protect Hazel.

The three girls came down the stairs each with a bag though Hazel had two because of mine. I hurried over to take it from her but then Luken and Oliver took all of them. Seconds later they were back inside.

"We're all set," Oliver told us.

Luken stepped into the middle. "We have a plan. Miller and the girls will go in his car. Caleb too like before since he can help. Dark magic fighting dark magic and all that. Oliver will follow with me behind him. That way if anyone comes up, we can distract them."

"That sounds good," Dad agreed. "But again, Miller, you don't stop until you're there."

"Got it."

Dad hugged me tightly and then slapped my back before I went over to Mom who squeezed me so tightly. "Be careful," she said against my chest."

"You know me, Mom."

When she pulled back she gave me a look that

made me laugh. "Yeah. I do. That's why I said be careful."

The guys chuckled as the girls tried not to. Especially Hazel.

Mom went around giving each of us a hug. Dad shook the guy's hands and gave last-minute tips. Then it was time to go.

We piled into our vehicles and more explosions rocked the town. It was so fucking weird to be running away from shit like that when for years, Luken, Oliver, and I had run toward it. But now, we had a different mission. One that was personally more important.

I sped off in the direction dad sent us while Caleb sat in the seat beside me whispering a chant and twirling his fingers. The girls held each other's hands in the backseat. The now familiar gray smokey haze surrounded us as his spell to help hide us from his former coven swirled around the car. I'm sure he did his best to include Luken and Oliver but as long as it kept the girls safe, that was what mattered.

It didn't take long for the shit to hit the fan. We were run up on. The spells being cast thudded against Caleb's protection. I hit the gas so that we could speed off. When there was a little distance between us and them, Luken went in one direction, Oliver in the other.

They were splitting up to force the shadow coven to dive themselves. They were easier to pick off when they weren't in a pack. A flash of light exploded behind us but I just pushed the car faster.

It took a while for us to get where we needed to go and luckily I didn't have to take any detours to throw the shadow coven off our backs.

Luken and Oliver had taken care of that and now I wanted to hear from them.

"Where are the guys?" Hazel asked, her jade eyes glowing in my rearview mirror.

After glancing at Caleb, I told her, "They'll meet us there."

"Yeah, but where are they Miller?" It was like she'd just realized they were no longer behind us.

"They split up to distract the shadow coven so that we can get you safe."

Her eyes widened and her lips parted. "I don't want anyone hurt because of me."

Caleb turned in his seat. "You don't get to decide that. All of this is to protect you three and keep the shadow coven from trading you, raping you, or killing you."

Sure, it was a little harsh but it was all the truth and I wasn't mad about the way he told them.

"We need to trust that they know what they're doing," Gia told her. "Maybe once we're at this cabin, we can practice our own magic so that we won't be so reliant on them."

Yeah. That was going to happen. I wasn't going to leave these women defenseless like their parents had. Or like I kind of had with Hazel already. The same mistake wouldn't be made twice.

"Yeah." Hazel sighed. "We're definitely doing that."

It was surprising how fast you could get somewhere when you needed to. After breaking probably every traffic law that anyone had ever thought of, I pulled down an overgrown path. I couldn't even call it a drive and stopped when I couldn't go any further.

The five of us got out of the car and I took Hazel's hand as soon as I could. If I had her with me, I'd be able to stand between her and anything that came up on us. Caleb was behind me with Nellie and Gia.

We walked in the direction we were supposed to and after only a few feet, the zap of a powerful ward tingled over my skin. We'd entered the runes. But shit...

Caleb wouldn't—

His scream echoed through the forest causing a few birds to flap away. "Drink the potion," I told him but he was on the ground trying to catch his breath.

Releasing Hazel's hand, I left her there to step back through the rune. He wouldn't have heard me because of the protection.

I reached out a hand to help him up. He was breathing like he'd just been on a run. "You have to drink the potion to hide the dark magic from the runes."

"Right. Fucking forgot." He pulled the bottle out of his pocket and drank. Then he was able to step through into the protected area.

"You won't be unloading the cars," I told him. "Don't want to waste the potion with that many trips through."

"Yeah." He nodded. "I guess we know it fucking works."

I snorted. "I mean, I was just going to trust that it did but didn't think about you not making it through."

"This place is beautiful." Hazel was gazing around though we hadn't gone inside.

"It is." I marched back over to her. "It's going to be home for a bit so we'd better get this place opened. If Mom and Dad haven't been up here, there's probably some cleaning that needs to be done. If you four start on that, I'll get the shit from the car."

I headed that way right as we hear more vehicles and I stopped mid-step. Everyone froze as we waited. It had to be Oliver and Luken. Had to be but until we saw them and were sure, I wasn't moving.

After several strained heartbeats, the two of them stepped out of the woods into the clearing as they laughed. They saw us all standing there and smiled. Obviously, light witches could see through the runes.

"We took care of them," Luken assured me as they stepped through the ruins.

"One fucker got away," Oliver said. "But the others…"

At least there was that.

Quickly the three of us got the cars unpacked and when I entered the cabin, Caleb was showing the girls some basic spells to tidy up the cabin.

"Fuck." Luken fell through the door. "That bastard that got away followed us. Saw us at the car." He dropped the bags he hand while Caleb, Luken, and I joined Oliver outside.

I looked back at the girls. "Stay here."

This was going to be the first test of the ruins.

The four of stood outside on alert, listening to the rustle in the woods. Each of us ready to fight at a moment's notice.

When the single mad stepped out, a black haze emanating from his hand, we waited.

Because there was one thing I knew...

No one was getting through me. I was going to protect Hazel with my life.

FATED MAGIC

THE SHADOW COVEN BOOK 3

Now that Hazel's back, not even the darkest magic will get to her...

After getting out of the dark magic camp for women whose parents have promised them as payment for a debt, we have a lot going on.

Miller discover that his family has secrets. Secrets that make him ready to kill.

My parents have promised me to a dark Face that is hell bent on receiving his payment.

We're in hiding, yet even that doesn't promise security.

All around us there's danger. Miller is ready to kill at every turn.

A fight is coming and I'll be ready to defend those that I love.

I you'd like to just keep up with my sales and new releases, you can follow me on BookBub!

Bookbub: https://www.bookbub.com/authors/ heather-young-nichols

About the Author

Heather Young-Nichols is a USA Today Bestselling author of contemporary and paranormal romance. A native of the great and often very cold state of Michigan, she is better known at home and to her friends as the Snarker-in-Chief. A job she excels at beyond anything she could have imagined. She loves many things, but especially cold coffee, hot books, and baseball. But not necessarily in that order.

Find Heather on Social Media or by visiting her website.

heatheryoungnichols.com

facebook.com/heatheryoungnicholsauthor

instagram.com/heatheryoungnichols

amazon.com/Heather-Young-Nichols/e/B00KKTM54A

bookbub.com/authors/heather-young-nichols

tiktok.com/@heatheryoungnichols